- 中央高校基本科研业务费专项资金资助课题"认知语言学视角下的外语习得研究"（2017JDZD08）阶段性研究成果
- 江南大学人文社科研究基地"钱锺书及其海外传播研究中心"资助
- 江南大学人文社科研究基地重点项目"新媒体背景下的翻译与文化传播研究"(2019JDZD17)阶段性研究成果

格式塔理论视角下散文翻译中的意象再现研究

A Study of Image Reproduction in the Translation of Literary Essays from the Perspective of Gestalt

李 梦 龚晓斌 著

苏州大学出版社
Soochow University Press

图书在版编目(CIP)数据

格式塔理论视角下散文翻译中的意象再现研究 / 李梦, 龚晓斌著. —苏州:苏州大学出版社, 2019.6(2020.5 重印)
ISBN 978-7-5672-2798-9

Ⅰ. ①格… Ⅱ. ①李… ②龚… Ⅲ. ①散文-英语-文学翻译-研究-中国 Ⅳ. ①Ⅰ207.6②H315.9

中国版本图书馆 CIP 数据核字(2019)第 082417 号

书　　名:	Geshita Lilun Shijiaoxia Sanwen Fanyi zhong de Yixiang Zaixian Yanjiu 格式塔理论视角下散文翻译中的意象再现研究 A Study of Image Reproduction in the Translation of Literary Essays from the Perspective of Gestalt
著　者:	李　梦　龚晓斌
责任编辑:	杨　华
装帧设计:	刘　俊
出版发行:	苏州大学出版社(Soochow University Press)
社　　址:	苏州市十梓街1号　邮编: 215006
网　　址:	www.sudapress.com
邮　　箱:	sdcbs@suda.edu.cn
天　猫　店:	https://szdxcbs.tmall.com
印　　装:	虎彩印艺股份有限公司
邮购热线:	0512-67480030
销售热线:	0512-67481020
开　　本:	890mm×1240mm　1/32　印张: 6.75　字数: 150 千
版　　次:	2019 年 6 月第 1 版
印　　次:	2020 年 5 月第 2 次印刷
书　　号:	ISBN 978-7-5672-2798-9
定　　价:	35.00 元

凡购本社图书发现印装错误,请与本社联系调换。服务热线: 0512-67481020

自 序

自 序

　　本书主要从格式塔理论角度研究散文翻译中的意象再现问题。散文素有"美文"之称，灵动飘逸，作者在表达思想情感时不必拘泥于形式。古今中外，文坛名家们创造出无数脍炙人口的散文，他们或于青山绿水中感悟人生哲理，或于记人记事中抒发内心情感，或针对某一具体话题发表真知灼见，文采斐然，内涵丰富，文学价值甚高。近现代以来，一些翻译家为了将散文大家的思想光芒在世界范围传扬，已经系统地整理编译出名家散文选集，极大地方便了海内外读者探索世界散文宝库。与散文创作及其翻译实践的蓬勃发展相比，针对散文翻译的研究较为滞后，系统研究较少。

　　对于文学翻译的研究，从传统的语言学派到文化转向，从文本研究到译者风格研究，相邻学科的概念借鉴极大地影响着翻译研究的发展。文学文本有别于其他类型的文本，不仅传达文字意义，更蕴含独特的审美体验。因此，近些年来，一些学者借鉴美学和心理学相关研究，为翻译研究提供了新的方向。其中，格式塔心理学和格式塔意象再造理论的贡献较为突出。格式塔心理学从心理学角度,强调经验和行为的整体性,提出人在视知觉感知时遵循整体原则、异质同构论、图形-背景分离原则、接近原则、相似原则、闭合原则和连续原则,这些主张有助于研究译者在翻译过程中的心理操作。格式塔意象再造理论基于格式塔心理学的完形趋向律法则,从美学角度研究文学翻译,主张文学翻译不是逐字逐句的机械对应,而是格式塔意象的再造。原文本中有很多意象,它们所蕴含的审美体验并不是直接存在的,也不是看到即得来的。因此,译者并不能由简单的"刺激-反应"直接得出译文,而是需要进行中介处理,即先将原文中由个体意象融合而成的格式塔意象进行心理再现,然后再将其用译文语言进行再造。

  本书将格式塔心理学与格式塔意象再造理论相结合,以张培基译注《英译中国现代散文选》、卜立德译《古今散文英译集》、夏济安译《美国名家散文选读》、高健译注《英美散文名篇精华》、刘士聪编著《汉英英汉美文翻译与鉴赏》为研究对象,从中译英和英译中两个方向,研究散文翻译中的意象再现,并对比散文中译英和英译中时意象再现的异同。

  本书主要采用文献研究法,查找并研读散文中译英、英译中相关文献,包括指导理论和研究对象。写作前,作者充分研读所用理论专著及上述五位译者的散文选,结合前人研究的总体情况,提出新的问题,并尝试解决。在主体分析中,本书主要采用例证法,从中译英、英译中两个方向证明格式塔理论对散文翻译中意象再现的指导作用。

  本书首先介绍散文翻译中意象再现研究的背景、意义、

自序

目的和本书结构,然后综述散文翻译及格式塔理论在翻译中应用的研究现状,提出目前研究的不足之处。接下来阐述格式塔心理学的基础原则,以及格式塔意象再造理论对翻译过程和审美效果的阐释,从格式塔理论角度提出一个相结合的方法,为散文翻译中的意象再现研究提供一个新的衡量标准。在具体分析时,本书运用这一标准衡量张培基、卜立德、夏济安、高健、刘士聪编译的散文选中的意象再现,从中译英、英译中两个方向在词汇、结构和审美层面对译文语言进行对比分析,融入对译者的翻译策略的探讨,为散文翻译研究提供借鉴。

研究发现,格式塔心理学基本原则确实可以与格式塔意象再造理论相结合,新的方法以格式塔原则为影响译者翻译操作的主要动力,以格式塔意象再造理论的三大美学效果(即词汇、结构和审美体验)为衡量层面,对中译英、英译中时的意象再现均可提供指导作用。具体来说,一个格式塔原则至少可以应用于词汇、结构、审美中的一个层面,帮助译者更好地再现个体意象,从而成功再造原文格式塔意象所创造的氛围和情感。新方法的优势体现在两个方面:一是阐明了格式塔原则就是译者形成格式塔意象的心理动力;二是证明了除闭合原则之外,其他格式塔基本原则也对意象再现有着重要的指导作用。另外,译者在英译中和中译英时都会运用闭合原则、整体原则来选择恰当的词汇,运用整体原则、连续原则和图形-背景分离原则来创造和谐的文章结构,运用异质同构论、接近原则和闭合原则来更明确地表达和再现原文的总体氛围,传达作者的情感。

就译者所采取的具体策略和美学效果而言，在词汇层面，虽然格式塔理论支持两个方向的译者对词汇性质和意义进行调整和补充，但英译中时四字词的运用不仅使词汇意义变得完整，还对其进行了延伸，使意象的再现完善且富有美感。在结构层面，两个方向的译者都以格式塔意象和话题为核心，对句子结构进行调整，但中译英往往将短语简化，融入英文长句，英译中则相反。在审美体验层面，两个方向的译者都通过对格式塔原则的运用，成功再现了原文格式塔总体意象的情景氛围和情感，但英译中时四字词和半文言的运用增添了译文语言的古朴韵味。

　　本书的研究意义在于从格式塔理论角度探讨了散文翻译中的意象再现，结合格式塔心理学原则和格式塔意象再造理论，包含中译英和英译中两个方向，为这一角度的散文翻译研究提供了较为系统的结构。另外，本书中的分析也从格式塔理论角度融入了译者的翻译策略，为翻译实践提供了新的视角。

　　本书的创新点在于将格式塔心理学原则与格式塔意象再造理论相结合，一定程度上丰富了散文翻译中意象再现研究的格式塔理论视角。另外，从中译英和英译中两个方向来研究散文翻译中的意象再现，打破了之前只对一个系列的散文选集进行个案研究的局限。

　　谨此为序。

李　梦　龚晓斌
2019 年 5 月于江南大学

Preface

The present study explores the image reproduction in literary essay translation from the perspective of gestalt. Literary essays enjoy the reputation for "aesthetic writing" because of their flexibility and elegance in supporting the authors to express their thoughts and feelings freely without constraint by the form of expression. Throughout the world all the time, literary masters have created abundant literary essays that enjoy great popularity. They comprehend the philosophy of life in the beautiful scenes of nature, narrate past events and persons to express rich emotions, or comment on certain topics, which sparkles with the light of wisdom and is of high literary talent. In modern times, some famous translators at home and abroad have systematically collected and translated outstanding literary essays into anthologies in order to promote them and enable readers throughout the world to get access to the repository of literary essays. Compared to the prosperous development of literary essay writing and translation practice, researches on literary essay translation fall behind with few systematic studies involved.

Researches on literary translation have experienced the change from the traditional linguistic school to the cultural turn with research topics including not only the text but also the translator's style, which indicates the power of drawing from adjacent disciplines. One characteristic differing literary texts from other texts is that the former convey not only linguistic meaning but also unique aesthetic experience. Therefore, researchers recently have drawn on the concepts of aesthetics and psychology to provide literary translation with a new direction, among which, gestalt psychology and the theory of image-G actualization make the most prominent contributions. Gestalt psychology emphasizes "the wholeness in experience and behavior", proposing that the visual perception of human beings follows the principle of wholeness, heterogeneous isomorphism, principle of figure-ground segregation, principle of proximity, principle of similarity, principle of closure and principle of continuity. These principles support researchers to explore the translator's mental operation during translation. The theory of image-G actualization is based on the gestalt law of prägnanz and explores literary translation from an aesthetic perspective. It advocates that literary translation is not the linguistic word-for-word correspondence; instead, it is the reproduction of gestalt images. Images in the source text contain not only linguistic meaning but also aesthetic experience that is embedded in the language and cannot be directly obtained by a person the minute he reads. Therefore, the translator cannot reach the translated text through direct "stimulus-response". An intermediate operation is needed. During translation, the translator firstly mentally actualizes the image-G constituted by individual images of the source text, and then he can reproduce the image-G in the target language.

This research attempts to combine gestalt psychology with the theory of image-G actualization. Research objects include Zhang Peiji's four volumes of *Selected Modern Chinese Essays*, David Pollard's *The Chinese Essay*, Xia Ji'an's *A Collection of American Essays*, Gao Jian's *A Collection of British and American Essays* and Liu Shicong's

Prose Translation and Appreciation. This book explores the image reproduction in both C-E and E-C literary essay translation and conducts a comparison between them from a gestalt perspective that combines gestalt psychology and the theory of image-G actualization.

The main research method the present study adopts is literature study. At an early stage, literatures concerning researches on both C-E and E-C literary essay translation provide the present study with the current situation of literary essay translation study, including the guiding theory and research object. Before the writing is under way, reading of the monographs introducing theories adopted by the present study and five series of literary essay translation anthologies helps the authors put forward the research questions based on the inspiration of former researches. In the analysis part of this book, exemplification facilitates the present study to solve the research questions and to prove the guidance function of the combined gestalt theory on image reproduction of both C-E and E-C literary essay translation.

This book at first introduces the background, significance and objectives of the research on image

Preface

reproduction in literary essay translation, followed by the outline of this book. It later reviews the current situation of researches on both literary essay translation as well as the application of gestalt psychology and the theory of image-G actualization in literary translation at home and abroad and finds the research gap. Then it elaborates seven basic gestalt principles as well as the translation process and aesthetic effects proposed by the theory of image-G actualization, incorporating them as a combined approach from the perspective of gestalt and providing a new criterion for the research on image reproduction in literary essay translation. Applying this criterion in analysis, this book selects typical examples from the five series of literary essay translation anthologies to explore image reproduction in both C-E and E-C literary essay translation at lexical, structural and aesthetic experience levels. Translators' techniques are also touched upon as revealed in the section titles, which sheds new light on literary essay translation from the perspective of gestalt.

  The present study proves that it is feasible to combine gestalt principles with the theory of image-G actualization. The combined approach adopts gestalt principles as the motives influencing the translator's operation and the three aesthetic effects (i. e. lexical, structural and aesthetic experience) as the evaluation levels, providing guidance for image reproduction in both C-E and E-C literary essay translation. To be specific, one gestalt principle can be employed at one of the three levels, facilitating the translator to successfully reproduce individual images and reappearing the atmosphere and emotion embedded in the image-G based on the source text. The advantages of the combined approach lie in two aspects. On one hand, it reveals that gestalt principles are the theoretical motivation in the mental actualization of image-G. On the other hand, it proves that other six gestalt principles, besides the principle of closure, are also influential to image reproduction in literary essay translation. What's more, the principles of closure and wholeness are instructive in helping the translator select appropriate lexical items; the principle of wholeness, principle of continuity and figure-ground segregation are enlightening in creating a harmonious structure; heterogeneous isomorphism, the principle of proximity and principle of closure are constructive in conveying the overall atmosphere and the author's emotion

Preface

of the source text more explicitly. When it comes to translators' linguistic techniques and their aesthetic effects, at the lexical level, although the combined gestalt approach supports the translators to change the word's part of speech and adjust and complete their meanings in both C-E and E-C literary essay translation, E-C translation's employment of four-character modules extends their meanings other than completion, enabling image reproduction to be comprehensive and aesthetic. At the structural level, both C-E and E-C literary essay translation follows image-G-oriented phrasal restructuring and topic pattern sentence progression, but C-E translation tends to simplify phrases into words and incorporate them in long English sentences while E-C translation conducts the opposite operation. At the aesthetic experience level, both C-E and E-C literary essay translation can reproduce the atmosphere and emotion embedded in the overall image-G based on the source text with the application of gestalt principles, but E-C translation's utilization of four-character modules and semi-classical Chinese adds antiquely refinement to the wording style.

The significance of this research lies in that it provides a fairly systematic study for image reproduction in literary essay translation from thet perspective of gestalt through connecting gestalt principles with the theory of image-G actualization and including both C-E and E-C translation. Moreover, translator's techniques are also incorporated in the analysis, shedding light on the translation practice of literary essays.

    The innovations of the present study lie in two aspects. To begin with, it combines gestalt principles with the theory of image-G actualization, extending the gestalt perspective on the study of image reproduction in literary essay translation. What's more, the research objects contain both C-E and E-C literary essay translation anthologies, breaking the limitation of only focusing on one series of anthology from one direction in previous studies.

Li Meng, Gong Xiaobin
May, 2019

Contents 目录

CHAPTER ONE INTRODUCTION / 1

1.1 Research Background / 3
1.2 Research Significance / 6
1.3 Research Objectives / 9
1.4 Outline of the Book / 11

CHAPTER TWO LITERATURE REVIEW / 13

2.1 Review of Research on Literary Essay Translation / 15
   2.1.1 Research on C-E literary essay translation / 15
   2.1.2 Research on E-C literary essay translation / 21
2.2 Review of Research on Gestalt Psychology and Image-G Actualization / 26
   2.2.1 Research on gestalt psychology and its application to translation / 26
   2.2.2 Research on image-G actualization and its application / 30
2.3 Summary / 35

CHAPTER THREE THEORETICAL FRAMEWORK / 37

3.1 Gestalt Psychology and Principles of Gestalt / 39
    3.1.1 Principle of wholeness / 42
    3.1.2 Heterogeneous isomorphism / 43
    3.1.3 Figure-ground segregation / 44
    3.1.4 Principle of proximity / 46
    3.1.5 Principle of similarity / 48
    3.1.6 Principle of closure / 49
    3.1.7 Principle of continuity / 50

3.2 Theory of Image-G Actualization / 51
    3.2.1 Gestalt images / 52
    3.2.2 Process of image-G actualization / 55

3.3 A Combined Approach / 62
    3.3.1 Image and image-G / 63
    3.3.2 The combination of gestalt principles and aesthetic effects / 68

CHAPTER FOUR AN ANALYSIS OF LITERARY ESSAY TRANSLATION FROM THE PERSPECTIVE OF GESTALT / 77

4.1 Image Reproduction in C-E Literary Essay Translation / 80
    4.1.1 Gestalt principles and aesthetic selection of lexical items: C-E / 81
    4.1.2 Gestalt principles and aesthetic harmony of

structure: C-E　/ 90
4.1.3　Gestalt principles and the consistency of aesthetic experience: C-E　/ 109
4.2　Image Reproduction in E-C Literary Essay Translation　/ 122
4.2.1　Gestalt principles and aesthetic selection of lexical items: E-C　/ 122
4.2.2　Gestalt principles and aesthetic harmony of structures: E-C　/ 134
4.2.3　Gestalt principles and the consistency of aesthetic experience: E-C　/ 144
4.3　A Comparative Study of Image Reproduction in C-E and E-C Literary Essay Translation　/ 156
4.3.1　Lexical level　/ 158
4.3.2　Structural level　/ 161
4.3.3　Aesthetic experience level　/ 164
4.4　Summary　/ 167

◻ CHAPTER FIVE　CONCLUSION　/ 171

5.1　Major Findings　/ 173
5.2　Limitations of the Study　/ 180
5.3　Suggestions for Future Study　/ 181

REFERENCES　/ 182
后记　/ 191

LIST OF TABLES

Table 4.1 The employment of gestalt principles in C-E and E-C literary essay translation / *157*

Table 4.2 Translator's techniques in linguistic expressions in C-E and E-C literary essay translation / *158*

LIST OF FIGURES

Figure 3.1 Figure-ground segregation (Jiang Qiuxia, 2002: 177) / *45*

Figure 3.2 Columns of dots (Evans & Green, 2006:66) / *46*

Figure 3.3 Rows of dots (Evans & Green, 2006:66) / *46*

Figure 3.4 Columns of shapes (Evans & Green, 2006:67) / *48*

Figure 3.5 A triangle and three black circles (Evans & Green, 2006:67) / *49*

Figure 3.6 Two rectangles (Evans & Green, 2006:67) / *50*

Figure 3.7 The image-based literary translation model (Jiang Qiuxia, 2002:35) / *56*

CHAPTER ONE

INTRODUCTION

CHAPTER ONE
INTRODUCTION

1.1 Research Background

When it comes to literary translation, much attention has been paid to poetry and fiction because poetry presents neat rhyme and form while fiction possesses a relatively complete plot. However, the research value of literary essays is high for that it not only enjoys the reputation for "aesthetic writing" but also enables writers to express their feelings in a free and direct way. Therefore, great writers throughout the world have created splendid literary essays all the time. Generally, literary essays are short in length but profound in meaning, ranging from informal essays, familiar essays, miscellanea, travelogues, diaries, letters, memoirs to reports. Current research on literary essay translation is creatively conducted from various perspectives, including translation aesthetics, translator's subjectivity, reader's response, the theory of cultural intervention, the theory of relevance and so on. Some of these perspectives borrow concepts from adjacent disciplines and broaden the field of translation studies, inspiring the present study in drawing on other disciplines to explore literary essay translation. As an indispensable part of literary translation, the translation of literary essays requires not only the representation of the source text's content, but also the embodiment of its aesthetic effects. This emphasis on the "wholeness" of the text corresponds to the statements of the theory of gestalt, consisting of gestalt psychology and the theory of image-G actualization. Gestalt psychology emphasizes the importance of the whole and proposes several basic principles of human perception. The theory of image-G actualization was proposed by Jiang Qiuxia in her monograph *Aesthetic Progression in Literary Translation: Image-G Actualization*, which combines literary translation with the gestalt principle of closure, putting forward a new model for the aesthetic progression of literary translation. Based on the gestalt perspective, they may shed new light on the study of literary essay translation.

CHAPTER ONE
INTRODUCTION

Throughout history, plenty of writers at home and abroad have created abundant amount of literary essays. Taking the era of writing and familiarity to readers into consideration, this research chooses modern literary essays both in Chinese and English as the research object. Therefore, literary essays in the present study refer to short prose writings in vernacular words. Among the extensive field of Chinese literary essay's translation into English, Zhang Peiji makes the most significant contribution. His four volumes of *Selected Modern Chinese Essays* constitute a relatively complete series of important modern Chinese essays concerning different topics, containing not only the source texts written in Chinese but also the translated texts translated by Zhang Peiji himself. With respect to English literary essay's translation into Chinese, Xia Ji'an and his *A Collection of American Essays* with both source texts in English and translated texts in Chinese have attracted the most attention of the translation field. Both series of anthologies are of high value because of successful image reproduction, but they are never researched together. Focusing on them and other three C-E and E-C literary essay translation anthologies, the present study intends to make a comparison between C-E and E-C literary essay translation in terms of image reproduction from the gestalt perspective.

1.2 Research Significance

The present study possesses both theoretical and practical significance. Theoretically speaking, it exemplifies the importance of the study of both C-E and E-C literary essay translation with abundant texts. Literary essays enjoy a good reputation for a long time thanks to the free form and rich feelings. They occupy an important position in literature both overseas and in China. As a result, the translation practice of literary essays has been prosperously conducted both at home and abroad. However, compared to literary genres like poetry, fiction and drama, research on literary essay translation is much less. At home, research is mainly conducted on C-E literary essay translation from perspectives like functional equivalence, reader's response, translator's subjectivity, translation aesthetics, descriptive translation study, the theory of cultural intervention and so on. Research on E-C translation receives less attention in China. Studies of literary essay translation abroad are general and indistinct with

CHAPTER ONE
INTRODUCTION

most of them either introducing Chinese and English essays to those who are not familiar with them or analyzing certain essayists. What's more, most of the studies abroad were conducted a long time ago instead of keeping pace with time.

When the studies of literary text's translation are reviewed from the gestalt perspective, it is found that some are based on gestalt psychology and some are guided by the theory of image-G actualization. Two theories are employed respectively. The present study tries to combine the basic principles of gestalt psychology and the theory of image-G actualization. Gestalt psychology enlightens scholars in the translation field to pay more attention to the dynamic process of translation. The principle of wholeness is the kernel proposition of gestalt psychology, asserting that the whole is different from the sum of its parts and the whole is prior to the parts. With the gestalt principle of wholeness, figure-ground segregation, principle of proximity, principle of simplicity, principle of closure, principle of continuity and heterogeneous isomorphism, researchers can employ a novel approach to literary essay translation. Jiang Qiuxia proposed the concept of image-G and established an image-based translation model on the basis of gestalt psychology and aesthetics. Image-G is an image in the gestalt sense: the overall image. The two constituents of gestalt qualities of image-G are the contour and the mood. The process of image-G actualization includes mental actualization, linguistic actualization and aesthetic effects articulated from image-G. It also offers an effective evaluation framework for the translation of literary essays. As stated above, translation researches under the guidance of gestalt psychology and the theory of image-G actualization both fall into the gestalt perspective with the latter drawing on the former, so they can be combined. The present study attempts to propose a combined approach based on them and to analyze both C-E and E-C literary essay translation, which extends the content of literary essay translation from the gestalt perspective.

Practically speaking, the present study will also involve the techniques that prominent translators employ in their translation practice based on image transference from the gestalt perspective, illuminating the practice of literary translation.

In summary, research on literary essay translation is not adequate in that studies of E-C translation are few. What's more, gestalt psychology and the theory of image-G

CHAPTER ONE
INTRODUCTION

actualization can be combined in literary translation. The present study will fill in these two gaps and they form the significance of the study theoretically. Practically, this study will shed some light on the practice of translation apprentices, trying to improve their translation skills.

1.3 Research Objectives

This research attempts to guide literary essay translation from the perspective of gestalt, incorporating gestalt psychology with the theory of image-G actualization. Based on this core standpoint, it intends to answer the following questions:

1. Is it feasible to combine the analysis model under gestalt principles and the image-based translation model proposed by Jiang Qiuxia to evaluate literary essay translation? If yes, how does this combined approach operate and what are its advantages?

2. What aesthetic effects do the selected translated texts achieve evaluated from the perspective of gestalt? And how do they achieve these effects?

3. What are the differences between the functions of the combined approach to C-E translation and E-C translation?

In a word, this research tries to evaluate literary essay translation from the perspective of gestalt. Combining gestalt psychology and the theory of image-G actualization, it extracts the main idea of image transference from the theory of image-G actualization, analyzing the effects of good literary essay translation from the perspective of gestalt. At the same time, it adds gestalt principles into the intermediate mental operation of the translator, examining the techniques that excellent translators employ. Throughout the analysis part, this research uses examples of both C-E and E-C literary essay translation, making a comparison between the influences of the combined approach on these two directions. To sum up, it attempts to make a relatively comprehensive study of literary essay translation from the perspective of gestalt and guide common translators with the techniques employed by the selected prominent translators.

CHAPTER ONE
INTRODUCTION

1.4 Outline of the Book

This book contains altogether five chapters. Chapter One points out the background, significance, objectives and the outline of this research on image reproduction in literary essay translation from the perspective of gestalt. Chapter Two reviews literatures on both C-E and E-C literary essay translation as well as the applications of gestalt psychology and the theory of image-G actualization into literary translation at home and abroad, summarizing the current situation of literary essay translation and finding the research gap. Chapter Three illustrates the theoretical foundations of this research. It firstly explains the basic gestalt principles of gestalt psychology; then it elaborates the main content of the theory of image-G actualization, including the concept of image-G, the image-based translation model, the translation process and aesthetic effects resulted from image-G. Later it proposes a combined approach from the perspective of gestalt with gestalt principles as the underlying motives of the translator and three aesthetic effects in the theory of image-G actualization as the evaluation levels. Chapter Four analyzes image reproduction in both C-E and E-C literary essay translation with selected examples according to the criteria of the combined approach. Translator's techniques are also incorporated in the detailed analysis. In the last section of this chapter, a comparison between C-E and E-C literary essay translation in terms of image reproduction is also conducted. Chapter Five comprehensively concludes the present study on major findings and limitations; it also provides suggestions for future study.

CHAPTER TWO

LITERATURE REVIEW

CHAPTER TWO
LITERATURE REVIEW

This section consists of four parts: review of previous studies of C-E literary essay translation, E-C literary essay translation, the application of gestalt psychology into translation as well as the theory of image-G actualization and its implication.

2.1 Review of Research on Literary Essay Translation

2.1.1 Research on C-E literary essay translation

The practice of Chinese literary essay translation has been conducted for a long time in China and the achievements are fruitful, among which the most prominent ones are the four volumes of *Selected Modern Chinese Essays* collected and translated by Zhang Peiji. Also, research on Chinese literary essay translation inside China is prosperous and can be divided into four parts according to the content: research on certain famous literary essay translators, the comparative analysis of different translated versions of one literary essay, specific linguistic phenomena and artistic aspects during literary essay translation, and the literary essay translation study under the guidance of certain theories or perspectives. As to research on literary essay translators, Zhang Wenqing (2007) explores the translation thoughts and propositions of Zhang Peiji based on his monographs about translation study and theories, demonstrating with his translation practice in *Selected Modern Chinese Essays* and proving Zhang Peiji to be a successful translator and translation theorist. Sun Huifang (2009) makes a comparison between the translation style of Zhang Peiji and Liu Shicong, exemplified by Zhang's *Selected Modern Chinese Essays* and Liu's *Prose Translation and Appreciation*. The conclusions are as follows: similarities include appropriate wording, flexible sentence structures, considering the whole text, and similar artistic conception to that of the source text;

CHAPTER TWO
LITERATURE REVIEW

dissimilarities include different translation units and different translation techniques concerning sentence groups. In terms of the comparative analysis, Xin Chunhui (2005: 43-46) compares the translated versions of Zhu Ziqing's *The Transient Days* produced by Zhang Peiji and another translator Zhang Mengjing in terms of the form and content at levels of phonology, structure and meaning, arriving at the conclusion that Zhang Peiji's translation is better at all three levels in that it combines the form and content as an integrated whole. Shi Meilin (2015) compares three translated versions of *The Peanut* produced by Liu Shicong, Zhang Peiji, Yang Xianyi and Gladys Yang from the perspective of reader's response, proving that the target reader's response of the translated texts is considered by the translators through the employment of some translation strategies. When it comes to research on specific linguistic phenomena and artistic aspects, Tang Yaocai (2001: 57-62, 86) analyzes the cross-sentence translation strategy and comments on Zhang Peiji's literary essay translation from this aspect, finding that the most frequently used sentence structures in the translated texts are the compound sentence, the adverbial clause of time and the non-restrictive attributive clause. Yu Dong and Liu Shicong

(2014:92-96) focus on the rhythm in literary essay translation that was paid less attention to than the meaning and style, concluding that the rhythm serves to strengthen the author's emotion and to convey the thematic thoughts. Peng Fasheng (2016:128-138) emphasizes the guidance of the subject motivation principle in C-E literary essay translation, pointing out that the translator should recognize the stability of the subject and the orderly change of subjects at the syntactic level. Many researchers also employ various theories to guide the study of literary essay translation with one series of translated work as the research object. Zhao Yali (2009) explores the essay translation practice of Zhang Peiji from the perspective of translator's subjectivity, drawing the conclusion that this perspective is appropriate to research Zhang Peiji's translation not only in macro aspects like the selection of original texts, purposes of translation and translation strategies but also in micro aspects including the operation at lexical, syntactic and rhetorical levels of texts. Lai Xiaopeng(2009) comments on the aesthetic representation of Zhang Peiji's *Selected Modern Chinese Essays* from the perspective of translation aesthetics, providing an in-depth analysis of the translated texts at phonetic, lexical, syntactic and cultural levels. Wang Jun (2010) employs universals of translation in descriptive translation study to evaluate Zhang Peiji's translation, discovering that universals do exist in Zhang's translation and resistance to universals reveals his subjectivity in not being constrained by the original texts. Jiang Dandan (2011) concentrates on the study of modern Chinese prose translation under the guidance of Nida's theory of equivalence and proposes several translation strategies according to functional equivalence. Ma Jin and Jia Dejiang (2011: 370-374) apply the reader's response theory to analyze Chinese literary essay translation and put forward such macro translation strategies as considering the reader's language custom, understandability and aesthetic standards. Tang Ping (2015) conducts translation criticism on Zhang Peiji's translated versions of modern Chinese literary essays from the perspective of cultural intervention, pointing out that modern Chinese literary essay translation needs to follow the principle of "foreignization".

When it comes to C-E literary essay translation abroad, attention on Chinese literary essays is little. Although some translators have translated modern Chinese literary essays into English, the research on it is far from satisfactory.

Most of the research abroad is conducted by the sinologists or translators. Based on their translation practice, they carry out reflections and discussions about modern Chinese literary essays translated into English. Some scholars focus on Chinese literary essays, introducing and analyzing them as well as the essay writers. David Pollard, a veteran sinologist, has edited many representative Chinese literary essays of famous writers and translated them into English in *The Chinese Essay* in 2002. It encompasses not only the translation of these essays but also the detailed introduction of their writers, their thoughts and feelings as well as the translator's notes and reflections, which makes the book more like literary study. Pollard (1989: 81-98) also makes a comparison between English essays and Chinese literary essays. He points out some characteristics of English essays and concludes many essayist's evaluations about English essays and Chinese literary essays illustrated by examples. It is a tentative exploration of the similarities and differences between aesthetic standards of China and the West.

Some foreign scholars do research on the translation of literary essays. Hilarie Belloc (1931) puts forward six principles for essay (including fiction) translation in general

CHAPTER TWO
LITERATURE REVIEW

in his monograph *On Translation*, which also sheds some light on modern C-E literary essay translation. He emphasizes that the translator should regard the source text as a whole and not entangle in the words. He also proposes that the translator has enough rights to do some adjustments and transformations to create a target text that conforms to the idiomatic expression norms of the target language. Lucas Klein (2015) puts forward some suggestions for Chinese literary essay translation based on his own translation of *Notes on the Mosquito* written by a modern Chinese poet and essayist called Xi Chuan. According to Klein, "The writing makes the man, translation of style is based on the dissolution of self, and still involves re-creation and approximation." (2015:48) In other words, if the translator wants to retain the style of the source text, he should bring his own style into translation as little as possible. However, re-creation is also acceptable when it is necessary.

2.1.2 Research on E-C literary essay translation

In contrast with the blooming picture of Chinese literary essay translation research, study of English literary essay translation in China is not so much. The study falls into four parts: research on theories about English literary essay translation, famous translators of English essays and their translation styles and techniques, certain aspects of literary essay translation and strategies for them, and analysis of the practice of English essay translation under the guidance of certain theories. A few scholars research the theories about English literary essay translation. Zhao Xiuming and Zhao Zhangjin (2010) explore the history and characteristics of British and American essays and put forward some basic principles for literary essay translation from English to Chinese. Ma Dezhong (2006) discusses the criteria for English prose translation into Chinese, in which he studies Gao Jian's translation proposition that the tone and style of prose are translatable as well as Liu Shicong's theory of artistic flavor theory. Some researchers focus on famous English literary essay translators. Li Changbao (2008) comprehensively analyzes Wang Zuoliang's translation style in poetry, essay and drama translation. Qian Lingjie and Cao Ping (2011: 89-92) summarize the translation principles proposed by Liu Bingshan in three macro aspects, namely the translator's selecting source texts that he is interested in, possessing profound language, cultural knowledge and social

CHAPTER TWO
LITERATURE REVIEW

responsibility as well as conveying the style of the source text. Wang Bing (2014) researches the translation style of Xia Ji'an in his literary essay translation exemplified by Xia's *A Collection of American Essays*, pointing out Xia's translation strategies like sentence order restructuring and textual information addition. Several scholars put forward strategies for essay translation in terms of certain aspects. Xia Tingde and Ma Zhibo (2008:168-170) deal with the representation of prosodic elements in English literary essay translation, pointing out that the translator needs to realize that English is a stress-timed language while Chinese is a tonal language, to grasp the rhythm pattern of the source English text, and to reproduce it with the strengths of Chinese phonology under the overall atmosphere and emotion. Zhang Jiachen (2008:137, 140) focuses on the translation of plural nouns in E-C literary essay translation and puts forward four strategies, namely implicit mark conveying only the central meaning, explicit mark adding words to represent the plurality, adoption of the source text's expression form and blurring of the word's meanings. Zhang Jiguang and Zhang Zheng (2014:83-91) explore the norms for English literary essay translated into Chinese on the basis of corpus, proving that translator's strategies at lexical, syntactic and textual levels all follow certain translation norms. Many researchers explore the practice of English literary essay translation with the guidance of certain theories. Zhou Tao (2004:131-134) explores the aesthetic construction in English literary essay translation based on Xia Ji'an's translation of *The Old Manse* at the language, image and emotion levels. Wu Jianbo (2012) concentrates on the translation of English lyric essays under the guidance of the theory of transitivity, comparing the transitive processes of the source texts with the translated texts and reaching a comparison between them in regard to function. Huang Jianling (2012) makes a comparative analysis of three translated versions of Bacon's *Essays* from the aspect of translation aesthetics, focusing on the translators as the aesthetic subject in terms of their constraint to the original text and subjectivity in translation as well as the similarities and differences between the three versions at the phonological, lexical, syntactic and stylistic levels. Wang Xiaojing (2013) evaluates Xia Ji'an's *A Collection of American Essays* from the theory of relevance to prove that Xia achieves the optimal relevance between the translated texts and the target readers in that Xia employs fluent and understandable Chinese in

CHAPTER TWO
LITERATURE REVIEW

translation as if the translated texts are the source texts written in Chinese, maintaining the artistic features of the source texts and providing cultural knowledge for target readers of the translated texts.

There's little research on E-C literary essay translation abroad. Similar to the introduction of Chinese literary essays and essay writers, some foreign scholars introduce English essays of certain essayists. Tracy Chevalier has edited *Encyclopedia of the Essay* in 1997. This book generally defines "essay" as a literary genre that is a kind of nonfictional prose text. Thus literary essays are also involved. It covers essayists from various nations (including China but the majority is western), different categories of essays, influential single essays, and periodicals creating a market for essays and so on. In terms of the content, the alphabetically arranged entries usually encompass almost all aspects of the essayists or essays, such as biographical sketch, nationality, era, selected writings' list, additional readings, and anthologies. This book is therefore more of study than an introduction.

2.2 Review of Research on Gestalt Psychology and Image-G Actualization

The theory of image-G actualization is based on gestalt psychology, so it is necessary to review the application of gestalt psychology into the field of translation at first.

2.2.1 Research on gestalt psychology and its application to translation

The principle of wholeness in gestalt psychology has provided a new angle for translation study. Its main proposition is that the whole is not equal to the pure sum of its parts. It is prior to the parts and determines the nature and function of the parts. (Koffka, 1935) The most prominent scholar in China that introduces gestalt psychology into literary translation is Jiang Qiuxia. She proposes the concept of image-G and puts forward a model for its actualization during the process of translation. This will be reviewed in the following section.

CHAPTER TWO
LITERATURE REVIEW

Many researchers employ gestalt psychology as a perspective to study translation, applying common principles of gestalt psychology to evaluate and guide translation at the macro level. Most of them focus on the translation theory under gestalt psychology in general, paying attention to the dynamic process of translation or analyzing certain translators' propositions from the gestalt cognitive perspective. Zhu Guicheng (2008:67-72) raises hypotheses for translation with the employment of gestalt psychology in terms of some basic questions of translation, isomorphism, text movement and function of the unconsciousness. Tong Ying and Gu Feirong (2008:109-112) draw on the principle of wholeness, the principle of closure and heterogeneous isomorphism in gestalt psychology to analyze the translator's psychological activities during the process of translation, holding the view that the translated text is the integration of words, images and meanings. Through exemplification, they prove that the principle of wholeness is feasible for the translator's integrated thinking, the principle of closure is helpful for the reproduction of aesthetic images and heterogeneous isomorphism is instrumental to the translator's selection of appropriate source texts that fit his interest and characteristic.

Zhang Siyong (2011: 19-24) studies the translator Jiao Juyin's view of wholeness on translation under the guidance of gestalt psychology with the detailed analyses in terms of the principle of wholeness, heterogeneous isomorphism and figure-ground segregation. Some researchers apply gestalt principles to the translation of texts from specific fields, such as EST (English for Science and Technology) and brochures or introduction signs for tourists. Pan Weimin (2006:44-47) analyzes the English translation at Chinese scenic spots by employing the gestalt principle of wholeness, the principle of closure, figure-ground segregation, the principle of simplicity and the principle of continuity and improves the translated texts according to these principles. Wu Dilong and Zhu Xianlong (2008:74-77) discuss the translation of EST into Chinese with gestalt principles of proximity, similarity, closure and simplicity. Some evaluate literary text translation in terms of the application of common principles of gestalt psychology. Niu Rui and Chen Shanshan (2009: 84-87) examine the feasibility of gestalt principles to the analysis of the image translation in poems and novels written by authors both at home and abroad.

The most prominent scholar abroad employing gestalt

psychology into translation is Mary Snell-Hornby. She (1988) proposes that translation studies need to be considered as an independent discipline and puts forward an integrated approach based on German functional translation theories and gestalt psychology. In her monograph *Translation Studies: An Integrated Approach*, Snell-Hornby points out that "It is the holistic principle of the *gestalt* that will be essential in our integrated approach to translation, which for far too long was thought to be merely a matter of isolatable words" (1995: 28). When establishing a diagram of relationships between basic text-types and crucial aspects of translation, she (1995) also draws on gestalt principles and proceeds from the most general level at the top downwards the most particular level at the bottom. Therefore, isolated words and sentences are understood in a larger context within the integrated frame of the text. Farzaneh Farahzad (1998: 153–158) illustrates the translator's unconscious manipulation in the process of translation, employing two major concepts of gestalt psychology, namely pattern and pattern completion. The unconscious manipulation is the tendency of human perception to finish the incomplete as complete, facilitating the translator to fill in the blanks of the original text so that he can acquire a complete and comprehensive understanding of it. Pattern and pattern completion can be adopted by the translator as strategies in comprehending the original text as a whole concerning certain topics and following certain patterns and reproducing it in the target language.

2.2.2 Research on image-G actualization and its application

Image-G actualization is mainly applied to literary translation. According to Jiang Qiuxia and Quan Xiaohui (2000:26-30), as a form of art, literary texts contain aesthetic factors besides linguistic information. In the process of reading and comprehending the original text, the translator conducts the activities of language cognition and aesthetic experience. The translator makes comprehension of the original text based on these two activities and forms a gestalt image in mind. Finally he reproduces this gestalt image in the target language, and the transformation and actualization of both literary information and artistic factors can be achieved. They construct a model for the actualization of the gestalt image and point out that it doesn't make sense directly

CHAPTER TWO
LITERATURE REVIEW

achieving correspondence of words and sentences between the source text and the target text. The gestalt image as an intermediate schema is necessary, and the translator should absorb and represent the linguistic information and aesthetic factors as a whole. Jiang (2002) illustrates image-G actualization in detail in her monograph *Aesthetic Progression in Literary Translation: Image-G Actualization*. Later, research on image-G actualization springs up like mushrooms and most of the research focuses on literary genres like poetry and drama. Many scholars apply the theory of image-G actualization proposed by Jiang Qiuxia to conduct literary research. Meng Jin and Feng Dou (2005:91-94) explore the image-G of ancient Chinese poetry and propose a model for the transference of artistic conception during translation based on Jiang's theory of image-G actualization, examining poetry translation in terms of individual images, atmosphere, emotion and artistic conception. Wang Jianping (2005: 84-90) analyzes the fuzziness and blanks in ancient Chinese poetry and points out the significance of maintaining the gestalt qualities of the original poems. He draws the conclusion that some blanks need to be filled in; some need adaptation; some need to be retained as blanks in order to leave room for the reader's imagination in translation. Chen Gang and Li Genhong (2008:183-190) concentrate on drama translation on the basis of image-G reconstruction. They also build up a specific model for the procession of image-G reconstruction in drama translation.

Study of the theory of image-G actualization has not been found abroad, but many scholars have contributed to the formation and development of it. The contribution process can be divided into two parts: research concerning the image and models for translation. Miller (1986) points out the importance of image-visualization in literary translation. Lefevere (2004) explains the importance of the image in translation in that a book leaves an image to the reader after reading and translation is to transfer the image of a literary work into the target culture. Hatim and Mason (2001) assert that the translator should be constantly aware of the necessity to reconstruct the entire "gestalt" of the whole text out of the individual elements. Neubert and Shreve (1992) put forward a text-linguistic model rather than a linguistic model, which locates equivalence at the textual and pragmatic levels instead of the syntactic or lexical level. James S. Holmes (1978) also demonstrates a text-level literary translation model that contains a concrete serial plane where translation is the transformation from the source text to the target text based on sentences as well as an abstract structural plane where the translator generates a map in the source language, namely the mental conception of the source text and further evolves a map in the target language, according to which each sentence of the target text can be evaluated during the text reconstruction. After all, this model focuses on the linguistic schema and doesn't elaborate the mental process. Roger T. Bell (1991) refers to cognitive science and explores the black box of the translator's mental information processing as an intermediate operation. His model considers the source text as the information; then the translator analyzes the inputted source text through filtering, storage and recording and identifying its patterns, forming the short-term memory; later he integrates the individual parts of the source text into a whole in terms of semantic representation based on the acquired information during reading through coding the data stored in the short-term memory; finally he produces the translated text, transforming the input into the output and storing this information in the long-term memory. This model concentrates on the semantic whole and doesn't involve the aesthetic features of literary translation. Jiang Qiuxia doesn't agree that the translator forms two independent maps during translation and attempts to explore more on the aesthetic aspect that is different from former models on the cognitive aspect, so she presents the theory of image-G actualization for translation.

In research on literary essay translation from the gestalt perspective, scholars also fall into two systems. Some follow the theory of image-G actualization proposed by Jiang Qiuxia while some employ common principles of gestalt psychology as the standard. For example, Zhang Xiaohong (2011) explores the aesthetic representation of English literary essay translation exemplified by Xia Ji'an's *A Collection of American Essays* with the theory of image-G actualization as the criterion, evaluating the image actualization in the translated text in detail in terms of the aesthetic effect of harmony, coherence of image-G restructuring and selection of lexical items. Huai Yapeng (2010) focuses on modern Chinese literary essay translation with the employment of gestalt principles based on Zhang Peiji's *Selected Modern Chinese Essays*, examining the image reproduction in C-E literary essay translation and pointing out the guidance and requirements of gestalt principles to the translator.

CHAPTER TWO
LITERATURE REVIEW

2.3 Summary

Based on the literature review above, the present study finds the following blanks in the previous studies.

(1) The concentrations of the previous research on literary essay translation are either gestalt principles or the theory of image-G actualization, resulting in two different systems of research. The present study intends to combine them and to form a new approach from the perspective of gestalt.

(2) The research objects of the previous studies are single and insufficient in that they merely conduct case study of a series of translated works only in one direction either from Chinese to English or from English to Chinese. The present study encompasses both C-E and E-C literary essay translation anthologies and attempts to make a comparative analysis, adequately testifying the feasibility of the combined gestalt approach into guiding literary essay translation.

CHAPTER THREE

THEORETICAL FRAMEWORK

CHAPTER THREE
THEORETICAL FRAMEWORK

3.1 Gestalt Psychology and Principles of Gestalt

Gestalt psychology is founded in the 20th century by Max Wertheimer, focusing on human's perception of the external world. Wolfgang Köhler later enriches it by reflecting and criticizing certain propositions of structuralism. Kurt Koffka summarizes and develops the assertions of them and further raises common gestalt laws or principles of human perception. Altogether, they compose the core of gestalt psychology. "Gestalt" denotes the way a thing has been placed or put together; it is a German word. Its meaning lies in two aspects, namely shape or form as the characteristic of an entity, and "gestalt" is form in this sense; a concrete entity together with its specific shape or form as its attribute, and "gestalt" in this sense is any isolated whole. Taking the two meanings into consideration, "gestalt" seemingly refers to an entity as well as its form and attribute, but it isn't equal to "structure". "Structure" has its definition from the prevailing structural theorists, which differs from the essence of "gestalt". Therefore, Kurt Koffka adopts E. B. Titchener's translation "configuration" for "gestalt" in psychology. (Koffka, 1935)

Gestalt psychology emphasizes the wholeness of experience and behavior, opposing to the prevailing theories of structuralism that analyze perception by identifying the basic parts of broken elements or the "stimulus-response" formula of behaviorism. It advocates that the whole is not equal to the simple sum of its components and consciousness is not the collection of perceptual elements. (Koffka, 1935) These propositions derive from Max Wertheimer's discovery of illusion. In "Experimentelle Studien über das Sehen von Bewegung" ("Experimental Studies of the Perception of Movement"), Wertheimer (1912) discovers the phi phenomenon, an optical illusion that human mind presents in

CHAPTER THREE
THEORETICAL FRAMEWORK

which stationary objects shown in rapid succession appear to move. Because of the persistence of vision, pictures in rapid motion appear to present a moving scene to us. This finding proves the strong ability of human perception and provides the foundation for gestalt principles.

In *Gestalt Psychology*, Wolfgang Köhler (1947) criticizes introspection. Developing from the concepts of structuralist psychologists, introspection believes that consciousness could be understood by analyzing its elementary parts. Köhler (1947) claims that this proposition is too subjective and people tend to directly perceive the world as an organic unity instead of broken parts. People's experience is obtained from the relations of things in the world and they are stored as a whole scene in human mind.

Kurt Koffka (1928) finds that infants firstly perceive the world in organized wholes and only later can they perceive the separated components. He also adopts and develops the theories of Max Wertheimer and Wolfgang Köhler, holding the view that the natural experience we observe is gestalt-like. He (1935) elaborates common gestalt principles of people's organization of perceptual scenes in *Principles of Gestalt Psychology*, which is beneficial not only to the research of psychology but also to that of art and literature. This book will introduce seven gestalt principles in the next section, including two overall characteristics of gestalt psychology and five common perceptual principles illustrated through visual perception.

3.1.1 Principle of wholeness

The principle of wholeness is not only the kernel conception but also one of the two overall characteristics of gestalt psychology. Gestalt theorists put forward that what we perceive is greater than what we see. A component of any experiential phenomenon connects with other components, and this is why each component has its own attribute. All components constitute an organic whole, which is not dependent on one of its individual parts. However, the part is determined by the intrinsic characteristics of the whole. A complete phenomenon itself possesses wholeness, which cannot be dismantled into elementary parts and the attributes of the whole don't lie in the components. (Koffka, 1935) Altogether, the principle of wholeness has two implications. To begin with, the whole is not the pure sum of its parts;

instead, it is an integral organization of them which contains meaning and attribute that does not exist in its parts. The whole is primary to the parts, determining the characteristic and meaning of them. What's more, stimulus cannot directly lead to response. Human mind has an initial overall impression of the object we perceive and gives meaning to it as a whole.

3.1.2 Heterogeneous isomorphism

Heterogeneous isomorphism is the other overall characteristic of gestalt psychology. Gestalt theorists believe that the organization of the environment produces the same structure with the brain field of the person who experiences the environment. What's more, inspired by "field" in physics, Kurt Koffka (1935) proposes "psychophysical field" to denote people's mental activity, which is the integration of the psychological field and the physical field. The psychological field refers to the concept of people perceiving the external world; the physical field embodies the perceived reality. Although they are not strictly correspondent, their combination creates a holistic field, leading to the operation of human's mental activity. Later, Rudolf Arnheim (1954) applies it in the aesthetics of art, giving a further explanation about heterogeneous isomorphism. There is correspondence between the existing form of objects in the external world, people's perceptual organization activity, emotion, and the artistic expression of visual arts. Once the "forces" of these different fields reach the same operation in configuration, it provokes aesthetic experience. This is an important principle applied by many artists, poets and writers in their works from ancient times till today because it reveals the integration of the objects and emotions (or thoughts) in an artistic creation.

3.1.3 Figure-ground segregation

Figure-ground segregation is a typical perceptual principle raised by gestalt theorists. In a scene possessing certain configuration, some parts stand out and become the figure while some parts retire to the position of background as the ground. The figure is more easily to be perceived if the distinction between the figure and the ground is clear; it is the salient part that looks like a concrete object because of such definite distinctions. "Certain displays are bi-stable, in that what is perceived as figure can also be perceived as ground and vice-versa." (Todorovic, 2008:5345) It indicates that figure and ground are not absolute in certain scenes.

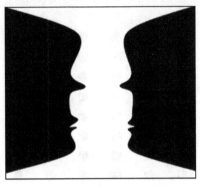

Figure 3.1 Figure-ground segregation

(Jiang Qiuxia, 2002:177)

As is shown in Figure 3.1, one may perceive the black parts as the figure and see two faces or consider the white part as the figure and see a vase with curves in the picture establishing the contour of the figure. Figure-ground segregation has two implications. Firstly, people's primary impression of a scene has a main focus. When one tries to retell it, a main subject is necessarily salient. Secondly, in a scene where both figure and ground have the prominent shape or salient characteristic, what is figure to some people may be ground to others. In this sense, figure and ground are mutually transferable on the surface structure.

3.1.4 Principle of proximity

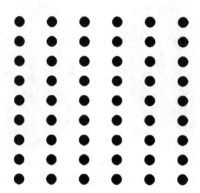

Figure 3.2 Columns of dots

(Evans & Green, 2006:66)

Figure 3.3 Rows of dots

(Evans & Green, 2006:66)

CHAPTER THREE
THEORETICAL FRAMEWORK

Gestalt theorists propose that some elements in a given scene are perceived as a group if they are close together. If the figure is divided into several sub-parts with a specific pattern resulting from proximity, people consequently perceive this figure into these sub-parts without deliberate efforts or concentrated attention. Once the form is arranged in a certain pattern, it attracts correspondent attention; the form is not the purposeful result of attention. (Todorovic, 2008) As is demonstrated in Figure 3.2, dots are closer together vertically and people can perceive six columns of dots without extra efforts. If one wants to naturally perceive these dots into horizontal groups, the picture needs to be rotated into Figure 3.3.

3.1.5 Principle of similarity

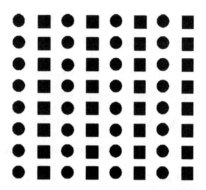

Figure 3.4 Columns of shapes

(Evans & Green, 2006:67)

The principle of similarity asserts that "Entities in a scene that share visual characteristics such as size, shape or color will be perceived as belonging together in a group" (Evans & Green, 2006:66). As is illustrated in Figure 3.4, although the distance between each adjacent circle and square is the same, people will not group them horizontally. Instead, one will see columns of circles and squares because the elements possess the same shape vertically. Sometimes the principle of similarity will be combined with the principle of proximity to strengthen the characteristic of the figure. The present study will explain this in detail in the following chapter.

3.1.6 Principle of closure

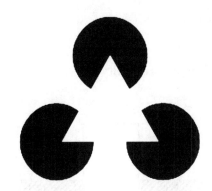

Figure 3.5 A triangle and three black circles

(Evans & Green, 2006:67)

Gestalt theorists claim that people tend to mentally perceive an incoherent, breached figure as a complete and intact one, and this is the tendency of closure that exists in people's perception. To put it simple, human perception tends to fill up the missing part of a relatively complete figure and recognize the incomplete as complete. (Evans & Green, 2006) In Figure 3.5, three imperfect black circles are demonstrated on the surface, but people tend to perceive the picture as a white triangle overlapping with three black circles.

This mental process suggests that people automatically fill in the blanks of a given scene. It also has a further implication: If the incomplete figures are purposely placed in a specific pattern, their blanks may create a new figure with a different shape and meaning.

3.1.7 Principle of continuity

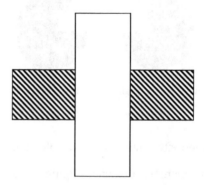

Figure 3.6 Two rectangles

(Evans & Green, 2006:67)

Gestalt theorists set forth that when a perceptual whole is formed, it remains continuously as a complete figure even when another figure intervenes through. The reason is that perception tends to prioritize continuous images. (Evans & Green, 2006) In Figure 3.6, although the picture displays a

CHAPTER THREE
THEORETICAL FRAMEWORK

white long rectangle and two short shaded rectangles on the surface, people tend to perceive it as a white long rectangle and a shaded long one crossing with each other because the shaded parts are considered as a continuous whole figure even with the interference of the white rectangle. The principle of continuity ensures the dominant place of the subject matter.

3.2 Theory of Image-G Actualization

The theory of image-G actualization deals with literary translation from the perspective of aesthetic. It is inspired by the gestalt law of prägnanz. This law advocates that human perception tends to present the perceived thing in good form, emphasizing more on the wholeness. Jiang Qiuxia (2002) illustrates the application of law of prägnanz in literary texts and puts high value on the groupings of parts of form a whole, during which process principle of closure plays a significant role for both the writer and the reader to link words together. The kernel concept of the theory of image-G actualization is image-G, namely a gestalt image which means an image in the overall gestalt sense. Before further analysis of this theory, it is necessary to introduce the gestalt image at first. Therefore this section will be composed of gestalt images and the process of image-G actualization.

3.2.1 Gestalt images

3.2.1.1 Image in the gestalt sense

Jiang Qiuxia (2002) points out that a gestalt image is a new concept of image deriving from the traditional image in literary genres like poetry and it is an image in the gestalt sense. The image in a literary text "refers to mental pictures produced out of language narration. It is to stir our imagination through a visual presentation of objects, persons and events" (Jiang, 2002:66). While the gestalt image refers to "the representation (mental and verbal) of a certain scene, a certain character or an event as a whole in a literary text … the author does not impose a linguistic pattern which only performs an informative function; rather he creates a sensuous world whose structure emerges in the perceptual act as various images" (Jiang, 2002: 67-68). The above statements suggest that the image and image-G contain the linguistic and

CHAPTER THREE
THEORETICAL FRAMEWORK

mental manifestations of a scenario, figure or event. Compared to the image, it is obvious that image-G is regarded as an overall complete contextual entity and is well integrated by the linguistic and aesthetic factors to present a unified idea. As a result, the overall gestalt qualities of the image-G are highlighted. An image-G in the literary text consists of a main idea as well as all elements composing this idea. It manifests two features: It builds up a pattern organizing the text, directing the textual meaning as a whole; it produces gestalt qualities like atmosphere and mood or tone. (Jiang, 2002)

3.2.1.2 Qualities of image-G

Qualities of image-G and the aesthetic effects created by its application in translation are two main aspects in the theory of image-G actualization.

Qualities of image-G include gestalt qualities and individual qualities. Gestalt qualities are composed by the contour as well as the mood or tone. The spatio-temporal background of a literary text sets the general foundation for its connotation and meaning. Connected with the topic and theme, they impress one with the contour of a whole pictorial image. (Jiang, 2002) In other words, the contour is the overall atmosphere constructed by the gestalt image in the text. It is the physiognomy or aura of the text that possesses particular attribute. The other integral gestalt quality of the image-G is the emotion or mood embedded in the literary text. It indicates the author's specific attitude or emotion toward the object and character in his text. (Jiang, 2002) To be specific, the mood or tone is the emotion or attitude the author conveys through the text, indicating the most significant expression of the object and character as well as leading to aesthetic experience greatly. Although these two components are explained separately, they are often combined in the presentation of a relatively complete image, incorporating the author's mood in language selection, structure rearrangement and producing a correspondent atmosphere. As a result, they form the two integral qualities of aesthetic experience.

Individual qualities of the image-G lie in individual linguistic items like sounds, words and sentences, or the analytical form. Linguistic items possess conventional meanings of their own, so they are often viewed independently. However, some of their aesthetic qualities can be activated only in the interrelation with the context. For instance, the sounds, words and sentences placed in a context can provoke reader's emotion through conveying aesthetic qualities like the affective tone. What's more, Jiang Qiuxia (2002) further points out that individual linguistic items also possess contextual meanings relying on the context they belong to and that the integrated contextual meaning influences the meanings of individual items in turn. Through such an interrelated relationship, individual items are also closely related to the image-G.

3.2.2 Process of image-G actualization

3.2.2.1 Image-based translation model

As is mentioned in the former chapter, Jiang Qiuxia (2002) puts forward a model for image-G actualization in literary translation based on the former cognition-oriented models as well as aesthetic theories. Literary translation is built upon the process of aesthetic image-G actualization. It is a process of image transference from the source text to the translated text constituted by two phases. Phase 1 is from the source text comprehension to a mental actualization of image-G; Phase 2 is from this mental actualization of image-G to a written linguistic actualization of image-G in the target text. (Jiang, 2002) This process can be explained in Figure 3.7 as the model for image-based literary translation:

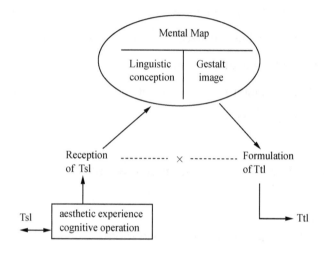

Figure 3.7 The image-based literary translation model

(Jiang Qiuxia, 2002:35)

In the above model, "×" in the dotted line suggests that this process cannot be achieved. "Tsl" means "text in the source language" and "Ttl" means "text in the target language". In the process of comprehension—representation of literary translation, the translator is not a subject automatically acting under the "stimulus-reaction" mode. In other words, the transformation from the source text to the target text is not achieved through the structural correspondence of their linguistic items such as words and sentences. The source text reception cannot directly lead to the target text production. Instead, the translator needs to employ his active function and constructs an intermediate schema—the gestalt image through constant interaction with the source text, and then transforms this image-G in the target text. Literary translation is not word-for-word correspondence but the overall reception and representation of linguistic meaning and aesthetic qualities. This model mainly deals with the aesthetic progression in the process of image-G actualization, including mental actualization, linguistic reproduction and the aesthetic effect of harmony.

3.2.2.2 Translator's mental actualization of image-G

Jiang Qiuxia (2002) illustrates that the process of image-G actualization includes: translator's extracting image embedded in the source text, translator's mental actualization of this gestalt image and translator's linguistic reproduction of image-G in the target text. Because of the dominant position of the translator in this process, Jiang not only preliminarily introduces the concrete operations of different parts in this process but also especially analyzes the role of the translator in Part Two of *Aesthetic Progression in Literary Translation*: *Image-G Actualization*. The present study tries to combine the mental process and the translator's perceptual operation in one section.

Jiang Qiuxia (2002) agrees with gestalt cognitive psychology that gestalt perception is an innate capacity. This capacity operates in literature as follows: When producing a text, the writer manipulates language to emphasize certain parts and pays less attention to other parts to outstand images and groupings; the reader can follow the direction of the language and actualize the image-G that the writer wants to convey. To be specific, there is a gestalt perception of image-G. After reading the source text, the translator (as a reader) can obtain a gestalt image in the mind through a process where he firstly obtains the contour. "Contour is the general yet rough idea one obtains at his first reading. The theme forms a vague image in the reader's mind as a contour. Other conceptions are then to enrich this contour and help to formulate a more and more distinct image. When contour realizes its proper richness, an image-G is fulfilled." (Jiang, 2002:186) Firstly, the translator acquires the basic contour

CHAPTER THREE
THEORETICAL FRAMEWORK

and emotion of the source text as well as relevant components that enrich the impressed image. When this image possesses enough richness, a gestalt image will be established.

Also, Jiang (2002) points out that during translation, if two languages share similar background knowledge and culture atmosphere, the translator will probably share similar schema with the writer. During the process of reading the source text, the translator feels the same way as the writer does, and finally the image transference can be achieved with less difficulty. However, when the two languages or culture backgrounds differ a lot from each other, it may require the translator to employ more active operations. Active operations include imagination as well as reflection and accommodation. Imagination assists the translator to combine those linguistic elements that are not associated or arranged in an equivalent position. (Jiang, 2002) This implies that in order to reproduce an image embedded in a source text whose surface structure is not so integrated in a consistent way, the translator needs to adopt imagination and figure out the underlying order and aesthetic qualities. Since the images built by the translator out of the first reading might be spontaneous and peculiar of the translator's own characteristic, reflection is necessary to improve the results of imagination, delivering a meaning containing more fidelity to that of the source text. (Jiang, 2002) Based on reflection, Jiang Qiuxia points out a further accommodation of a perceptual schema. The translator's accommodation of a perceptual schema can help him to "adjust his own schema to the original or the original to his own" (Jiang, 2002: 233). The assimilation of image-G structure resulted from accommodation ensures the comprehensive construction of an overall image in the translator's mind.

3.2.2.3 Linguistic actualization of image-G and aesthetic effects

The successful linguistic actualization of image-G in the translated text generates several aesthetic effects, among which harmony is the most significant. The translator can capture the overall gestalt image through the guidance of the harmonious schema in mind. Moreover, the mental actualization of this image-G in turn enables the translator to produce a translated text that conveys a harmonious effect. (Jiang, 2002) The function of harmony in literary translation rests on both the successful mental actualization of image-G and the aesthetic effects articulated from its linguistic actualization. Harmony is considered as the main feature to summarize the aesthetic effects created by the successful reproduction of image-G. When it comes to the application of harmony as a criterion, it is reflected first of all in the linguistic expression of the translated text. As artistic being, literary translation includes not only the transference of linguistic meaning but also the representation of aesthetic qualities. Therefore, the translated text needs to be examined at both linguistic and aesthetic levels.

After illustrating qualities of image-G and analyzing the image-G-oriented translation process, Jiang Qiuxia proposes the aesthetic effects of image-G on literary translation from three aspects. These three aspects together enhance the harmonious effect as is illustrated by Jiang Qiuxia (2002) as follows:

The effect of harmony rests on three facets. To begin with, image-G facilitates the translated text to be harmonious and natural in structure. This reflects that the translator needs to bear the source text as a whole in mind and reproduce it consistently; pursuing correspondence of the parts at the cost of losing the whole is inadvisable. What's more, the successful transference of image-G leads to effective transmission of aesthetic experience. If the translator can reproduce the contour and mood of a relative image-G, readers of the translated text can acquire similar aesthetic experience as those of the source text. Last but not least, image-G determines the selection of lexical items in the translated text. An individual word may have different counterparts in another language, but only according to the context (the whole) can the translator select the most appropriate one, which in turn effectively conveys the qualities of the whole together with other parts.

3.3 A Combined Approach

When conducting research on images in literary translation from the perspective of gestalt psychology, researchers tend to apply gestalt principles as the criteria. In the study of image-G in literary translation, scholars often adopt the theory of image-G actualization as the standard. Gestalt principles and the theory of image-G actualization are both based on the gestalt perspective, so the present study will

CHAPTER THREE
THEORETICAL FRAMEWORK

connect these two approaches and put forward a combined approach for literary essay translation. This approach will be illustrated in the following parts from two major aspects: the application of gestalt principles in the mental actualization of images as well as the three aesthetic effects resulted from the successful linguistic actualization of images. The combined approach starts with the connection between images and image-G.

3.3.1 Image and image-G

The image is a significant concept in literature, especially in poetry. Writers express their emotions implicitly through depiction of external objects, forming the basic manifestation of the image. Scholars in different times both overseas and in China have given different definitions and interpretations for the "image". Also, "imagery", the collective and assembly of images, is important in their definitions. Basically, their definitions are about images in poetry. In the early 20th century, imagist poetry thrived in western literature, whose founders T. E. Hulme and Ezra Pound both put forward statements about the image. Hulme firstly emphasizes in general that "images in verse are not mere decoration, but the very essence of an intuitive language" (Meng, 2004:2). Poetry records images comprehensively. Composed of different concrete and abstract images, poetry guides the reader's attention away from specific images to his imaginary mental process. Inspired by Hulme, Ezra Pound explains imagery as "an intellectual and emotional complex in an instant of time" (Eliot, 1954: 4). The combination of intelligence and emotion is highlighted in the image even though it reflects only an instant experience. Pound also implies that the literary text is connected to painting. Through subtle arrangements of words, sentences and even punctuation, the author intends to present an artistic visual image. (Jiang, 2002) T.S. Eliot further develops this statement into "objective correlative". To be specific, a series of objects and events should be the expressive form of that emotion so that the emotion can be evoked when external actions that trigger sensory experience occur. (Chang, 1990)

The discussions about "the image" or "*yixiang*" start in a very early time in China. Dating back to ancient China, Liu Xie firstly introduces "*yixiang*" to the field of literature in *Carving a Dragon with a Literary Mind*. Liu Xie firstly explains

CHAPTER THREE
THEORETICAL FRAMEWORK

the natural rule of people's emotions evoked by objects in the external world and then people write down their emotions and thoughts. Then he points out that an original and creative poet should create imagery according to the thoughts in his mind. This means when a poet selects words to express himself, the foundation is *yixiang* in his mind, which is the fusion of sensory objects and abstract concepts. Later in the Tang Dynasty, the famous poet Wang Changling advocates that in the process of creating a poem, a poet should explore among images with his heart roaming into the whole artistic conception. After this deep seeking, he can comprehend the objects and grasp the perfect ones to combine with his thoughts. Eventually he creates the image through a long journey in his heart.

The above statements about the image are mostly defined by poets, whose definitions of the image are in the classic and narrow sense. It is obvious that scholars both at home and abroad emphasize the fusion of author's emotion in the image. Also, these statements reveal the requirements of the image in cognition, aesthetics and literature. Cognitively, the writer needs to refer to his past perceptual experience and build up a mental picture of the image based on careful selection.

Aesthetically, the subtle arrangement of objects enables the artistic image to possess aesthetic properties. Literarily, the linguistic expression of the image embodies objects, events, thoughts, feelings and sensory experience. As is concluded by Jiang Qiuxia (2002), images in the traditional sense can be the presentation of a real external entity or the construction of a virtual, unfamiliar object. The former can be mentally produced by the reader through past experience and acquired knowledge, while the latter requires reader's imagination and further efforts in perception at the psychological level. (Jiang, 2002) However, images are of various types in literary forms other than poetry, as a result, the notion of the image needs to be broadened. Jiang Qiuxia puts forward a new concept for the image in the broad sense, "Image … is most comprehensive in that it means any piece of descriptive writing that can evoke mental pictures through visual imagination." (Jiang, 2002: 61) This is critical in identifying various images in literary essays, including not only the traditional ones that depict the surrounding scenes but also those hidden in the author's emotion. So long as a linguistic expression describes a scene, character or event and triggers pictorial imagination, it is recognized as an image. On the basis of this notion, Jiang

CHAPTER THREE
THEORETICAL FRAMEWORK

classifies images in literature into five types: "micro images: a. metaphor, b. symbol; macro images: c. scenes, d. characters, e. events" (2002: 63-64), which directs this research in selecting typical examples containing images.

According to Jiang Qiuxia, "An image-G can be constituted by a single word, a sentence, a paragraph or even a text ... So long as the sentence is isolated, it remains a final configuration; but the moment it is used with other sentences in paragraph building, it serves as an element in the paragraph configuration ... Thus image-G is a relative notion." (2002: 69) Therefore, if an individual image is analyzed separately, it can be considered as the minimal image-G and possesses gestalt qualities of contour and mood or tone. Conversely, if several individual images are combined together, they can create a larger image-G. In this sense, the image in present study draws on the qualities of image-G when analyzed independently and the scope of image-G can be broadened to relatively complete images.

3.3.2 The combination of gestalt principles and aesthetic effects

The translator undergoes two steps in the process of translation. The first step is reading the source text and forming the mental actualization of images and an overall image-G in mind. The second step is reproducing these images in the translated text according to the mental image-G and generating aesthetic effects as a result. The following section starts with the application of gestalt principles in the mental actualization of images and image-G.

As is mentioned in the former chapter, Jiang Qiuxia has agreed with gestalt cognitive psychology that gestalt perception is an innate capacity. An entity is perceived into an integrated whole; thus an overall image can be considered as gestalt. However, she just explains a few gestalt principles in text writing, not in translation; instead, gestalt perception in translation is explained from the point of human perception faculties. This is where gestalt principles can be combined with the theory of image-G actualization to explore literary translation. As is proved by Tong Ying and Gu Feirong

CHAPTER THREE
THEORETICAL FRAMEWORK

(2008:109-112), gestalt principles are feasible in analyzing the mental activities of the translator in image transference. Viewing individual images as dotted components, Su Chong (2017:272-289) draws on foreign scholar's research on gestalt perception laws' applications in the visual perception of natural images and proves their feasible employment in exploring the translator's mental experience of image-G transference in Chinese poetry translation. Inspired by Su, the present study considers individual images embedded in the text as component parts that can be integrated into an image-G through the translator's applications of gestalt principles during mental operation. Although the mental activities are in a "black box", they can be revealed in the translator's linguistic expressions. Different gestalt principles are employed to achieve the actualization of image-G in different types of texts and can produce aesthetic effects at the lexical, structural and aesthetic experience levels.

To begin with is the principle of wholeness. Gestalt theorists put forward that what we perceive is greater than what we see. Moreover, all components constitute an organic whole, which is not dependent on one of its component parts. However, the part is determined by the intrinsic characteristics of the whole. These are the kernel concepts of the principle of wholeness in perception. In literary translation, they have the following implications: individual images can form an image-G that possesses gestalt qualities resulting from the integration of them. Moreover, the gestalt qualities of image-G do not depend on an individual image; they determine the characteristics of the individual images. Therefore, the principle of wholeness influences the translator in the mental actualization of image-G, such as picturing the scenery as a whole through a bird's view; then he can conduct aesthetic selection of lexical items as well as harmonious arrangements of structures when producing the translated text in order to ensure that the atmosphere and emotion conveyed by the individual images are consistent with those embedded in image-G based on the source text.

Heterogeneous isomorphism believes that the organization of the environment produces the same structure with the brain field of the person who experiences the environment. As is explained by Arnheim (1954), there is correspondence between the existing form of objects in the external world, people's perceptual organization, emotion, and the artistic expression of visual arts. Once the "forces" of these different

CHAPTER THREE
THEORETICAL FRAMEWORK

fields reach the same operation, it provokes aesthetic experience. This principle is given full play at the aesthetic experience level in atmosphere reproduction in literary translation. To be specific, on the basis of mentally obtaining the atmosphere and emotion embedded in the image-G generated from the original text, the translator further achieves isomorphism with the author through aesthetic appreciation. Under such a circumstance, the translator incorporates the original atmosphere and emotion in linguistic reproduction of each individual image in the translated text by not only selecting appropriate meanings for certain lexical items but also restructuring according to the emotion conveyed by the image-G. Eventually, the target reader's aesthetic experience of the subject matter can be evoked when they reading the translated text.

Figure-ground segregation is a typical tendency of human perception according to gestalt psychology. In a scene possessing certain configuration, some parts stand out and become the figure while some parts retire to the position of background as the ground. The figure is more easily to be perceived if the distinction between the figure and the ground is clear; it is the salient part that looks like a concrete object because of such a definite distinction. The figure and the ground are not absolute in certain scenes and they are sometimes mutually transferable on the surface. In literary translation between Chinese and English, figure-ground segregation is mainly applied at the structural level. Since the sentence structure of English is like a tree where modifiers can be placed to any word in the main clause while that of Chinese is like a bamboo where a sentence consists of a string of clauses, the figure and ground of an image-G on the sentence surface can be at totally opposite positions. Therefore, the translator needs to recognize the true figure during the mental actualization of image-G, conduct restructuring in order to highlight the salient image of the image-G as the figure, and place the inconspicuous image of the image-G at the position of ground. Through such image reproduction, the image-G articulated by the source text can be successfully transferred into the translated text.

The principle of proximity is also one of the significant principles in gestalt psychology. Gestalt theorists propose that some elements in a given scene are perceived as a group if they are close together. In literary translation, it is often applied at the structural level. Because of the sentence features

CHAPTER THREE
THEORETICAL FRAMEWORK

mentioned above, both English and Chinese literary essays contain long complex sentences with many commas. With the help of this principle, the translator can recognize an image more appropriately, on the basis of which, he can successfully actualize the image-G integrated by individual images during the mental process and represent it in the translated text with a harmonious configuration.

The principle of similarity claims that entities sharing certain features are inclined to be grouped together. (Evans & Green, 2006) This principle is always employed at the structural level in literary translation. In literary essays, if several phrases or sentences that contain individual images form parallelism, they will be grouped together as an image-G and such patterns and the gestalt qualities will be retained in the translated text with the help of the principle of similarity. Also, if several phrases describe the same aspect of an image, such as its motion or appearance, they are often grouped together through restructuring. The translator either retains the structure or restructures that of the source text based on these groups according to the image-G formed during the mental process. This principle can also be employed at the lexical level. Sometimes when there are abundant adjectives modifying one image, the application of the principle of similarity may support the translator to change part of speech of certain words on the basis of grouping them together according to the image they belong to in order to avoid redundant use of one kind of part of speech. The retaining and adjustment in image reproduction resulted from the application of the principle of similarity facilitate the translator to represent the image-G based on the source text in a harmonious and aesthetic way.

The principle of closure states that people tend to mentally perceive an incoherent, breached figure as a complete and intact one, and this is the closure tendency that exists in people's perception. It occupies the dominant place in filling in the blankness and indeterminate parts in lexical items and aesthetic experience in literary translation. Because literary essays support the authors to express their thoughts and feelings directly, translators tend to reproduce them completely and explicitly through the employment of the principle of closure after the adequate mental actualization of the image-G. On the aesthetic selection of lexical items, this principle supports the translator to complete the image embedded in concise words as a whole. It also helps the

CHAPTER THREE
THEORETICAL FRAMEWORK

translator cope with culturally-loaded words in using their meanings as their counterparts in the translated text. On the consistency of aesthetic experience, the principle of closure enables the translator to express the author's feelings more explicitly through addition in image reproduction after fully imagining the image-G based on the source text.

The principle of continuity advocates that when a perceptual whole is formed, it remains continuously as a complete figure even when another figure intervenes through. The reason is that perception tends to prioritize continuous images. (Evans & Green, 2006) This principle comes into full play in the translation of literary essays that depict changing scenes with the movement of the author. This kind of essays usually has an overall topic and the description of changing scenes is only the detailed exploration of this topic. Therefore, the translator needs to bear the general topic in mind and to adopt the principle of continuity to maintain the dominant position of the topic when the subjects of the changing scenes change on the surface structure. To be specific, the translator can maintain the overall topic through recognizing the spatial order in the description of the changing scenes, adopting the principle of continuity during the mental actualization of image-G to ensure that reproduction of these individual images serves the representation of the topic and conveys the gestalt qualities of image-G based on the source text with a clear structure.

To sum up, the present study raises a new approach that employs gestalt principles as the translator's underlying motives in the mental actualization of images and image-G based on the source text. Adopting the image as the main concept, the new approach combines the mental actualization of image-G, image reproduction according to image-G and its aesthetic effects in three aspects, further putting forward the following evaluation parameters: gestalt principles and aesthetic selection of lexical items, gestalt principles and aesthetic harmony of structure as well as gestalt principles and the consistency of aesthetic experience. The application of them will be exemplified in the following chapter.

CHAPTER FOUR

AN ANALYSIS OF LITERARY ESSAY TRANSLATION FROM THE PERSPECTIVE OF GESTALT

CHAPTER FOUR
AN ANALYSIS OF LITERARY ESSAY TRANSLATION FROM THE PERSPECTIVE OF GESTALT

This study attempts to analyze both C-E and E-C literary essay translation and make a comparison between them from the perspective of gestalt. As is illustrated in Chapter Three, this study has already put forward a combined approach to literary essay translation from the perspective of gestalt that incorporates gestalt principles and the theory of image-G actualization. Therefore, the following sections will analyze the selected typical examples of C-E and E-C literary essay translation respectively according to the combined standard. During the analyses, the techniques that the translators employ will also be revealed in the subtitles. In order to analyze literary essay translation more comprehensively, examples that the present study selects come from five series of literary essay translation anthologies, including four volumes of Zhang Peiji's *Selected Modern Chinese Essays*, David Pollard's *The*

Chinese Essay, Xia Ji'an's *A Collection of American Essays*, Gao Jian's *A Collection of British and American Essays* and Liu Shicong's *Prose Translation and Appreciation*. The first two are C-E literary essay translation collections, followed by two E-C ones. Liu's collection includes both C-E and E-C translation. What's more, some great essays are collected and translated in more than one book mentioned above. The present study will also make a contrast between the different translated versions.

4.1 Image Reproduction in C-E Literary Essay Translation

According to the combined approach, the image is the basic unit of literary translation. The process of the image transference includes both the mental actualization of the images of the source text and image-G based on it as well as the reproduction of these images in the translated text through the linguistic actualization of image-G. Therefore, the following analysis combines them, with gestalt principles as the underlying motives of translators and aesthetic effects resulted from image-G as the kernel framework. To be specific, analyses will be conducted at three levels: gestalt principles and aesthetic selection of lexical items, gestalt principles and aesthetic harmony of structure as well as gestalt principles and the consistency of aesthetic experience.

4.1.1 Gestalt principles and aesthetic selection of lexical items: C-E

Images are easily found in literary essays that depict scenes, where they occupy the majority of the texts and produce sensuous enjoyment if represented as a whole. Among the repository of scenery essays, scenes are either in the dominant place and become the subject matter or play the role of background that expresses the author's feelings. In both situations the selection of lexical items from the gestalt perspective is by no means word-for-word correspondence. Bearing "wholeness" in mind, the translator needs to embed a lexical item into the relatively complete image that it belongs to and to further connect this image with other images related to it.

4.1.1.1 Meaning completion

Only in the context of an image-G can a translator select the proper counterpart of a word and accomplish successful image transference. It is significant to depict a scene as a complete one to reveal gestalt qualities of this relatively independent image-G, which brings about the important application of the principle of closure.

Example 1

ST:

不逢北国之秋,已将近十余年了。在南方每年到了秋天,总要想起陶然亭的芦花,钓鱼台的柳影,西山的虫唱,玉泉的夜月,潭柘寺的钟声。(Cited in Zhang Peiji, Vol.I, 2007: 158)

TT:

It is more than a decade since I last saw autumn in the North. When I am in the South, the arrival of each autumn will put me in mind of Peiping's Tao Ran Ting with its reed catkins, Diao Yu Tai with its shady

CHAPTER FOUR
AN ANALYSIS OF LITERARY ESSAY TRANSLATION FROM THE PERSPECTIVE OF GESTALT

> willow trees, Western Hills with their chirping insects, Yu Quan Shan Mountain on a moonlight evening and Tan Zhe Si with its reverberating bell. (Zhang Peiji, Vol. I, 2007:162)

The source text depicts five peculiar scenes of Peiping, the author's hometown, through which the author conveys deep affection for its autumn after ten years' departure with the first sentence setting the tone of nostalgia. The translator employs the principle of closure in order to mentally complete the five individual images and to fully reproduce the overall atmosphere of beautiful scenery in Peiping's autumn and the author's affection embedded in the image-G based on the source text. The linguistic expressions of the five individual images in the source text depict the representative scenes of beautiful scenic spots in Peiping in a conclusively concise way. In order to let foreign readers recognize that these places are in Peiping, the translator adds "Peiping's" in front of these places. What's more, "钟声" is translated into "reverberating bell" instead of word-for-word "bell", adding "reverberating" to reproduce the solemn echo of this Chinese temple bell that the author intends to convey and compensating from auditory sense of the vivid autumn scene of Peiping. Descriptions of these five images are of the same pattern in the source text, but the translator changes that of the fourth one "玉泉的夜月" into "Yu Quan Shan Mountain on a moonlight evening", which not only reduces the aesthetic boredom of repetition but also reaches the effects of emphasizing both the mountain and the moon and creating an integrated scene. The five individual images in the translated text together reproduce the relatively complete autumn scenery of places of interest in Peiping with both visual and auditory senses, successfully conveying the atmosphere of comprehensive beauty of Peiping's autumn and the author's nostalgia.

To sum up, when a lexical item depicting an image that contains abundant underlying sub-images, the translator needs to acquire an imagination of this image in mind and employ the principle of closure to complete it. In the process of the linguistic actualization of this image in the target language, the translator needs to reproduce it according to the author's feelings as well as other images surrounding it. Then the translator can select the proper counterparts of lexical items and they in turn can reproduce the overall atmosphere and the

CHAPTER FOUR
AN ANALYSIS OF LITERARY ESSAY TRANSLATION FROM THE PERSPECTIVE OF GESTALT

author's feelings as a whole.

4.1.1.2 Meaning adjustments

"In the reproduction of the text, one has to change the elements or differently integrate the same elements in order to modify the totality." (Jiang, 2002: 70) This statement indicates the reasonability in adjusting the components so as to correspond to the characteristics of the whole. When meaning completion cannot meet the requirements of reproducing the atmosphere and emotions embedded in a relatively complete image, it is necessary for the translator to conduct meaning adjustments according to the context. This is where the principle of wholeness comes into play.

Example 2

ST:

天空一片灰暗,没有丝毫的日光。

海水的<u>蓝色浓得惊人</u>,舐岸的微波吐出群鱼<u>喋嚅的声韵</u>。

这是暴风雨欲来时的先兆。

海中的岛屿和乌木的雕刻一样静凝着了。

我携着中食的饭匣向沙岸上走来,在一只泊系着的渔舟里面坐着。

　　一种淡白无味的凄凉的情趣——我把饭匣打开,又闭上了。(Cited in Zhang Peiji, Vol.Ⅰ, 2007:128)

TT:

　　The sky was a sheet of murky grey, completely devoid of sunlight.

　　The sea was a ghastly dark blue. The gentle waves licking at the shore gave forth a humming sound like that of fish in shoals.

　　All that foreboded a storm.

　　Some isles in the sea stood quiet and still like ebony sculptures.

　　I walked towards the sandy beach carrying my lunch-box and sat inside a fishing boat moored at the seashore.

　　What an insipid and dreary scene! I opened the lunch-box only to have it covered up again. (Zhang Peiji, Vol.Ⅰ, 2007:129)

　　The source text depicts a whole scene near the sea before

CHAPTER FOUR
AN ANALYSIS OF LITERARY ESSAY TRANSLATION FROM THE PERSPECTIVE OF GESTALT

a storm, comparing it to traditional Chinese inkwash painting that often consists of grey and black colors. This generally helps the author to establish the tone of depression. With abundant individual images, this excerpt creates a dreary atmosphere of the seashore surroundings which can be divided into two correlated parts and connected together by "I" in the context. One part includes individual scenery images arranged spatially that constitute the general background of a seashore awaiting a storm with both visual and auditory senses. The other part describes "my" inactive action under the general background. This implies that the principle of wholeness needs to be employed to connect the two parts in the translated text and all the lexical items constituting the scenery images of the environment need to be consistent with the author's feelings. As the translated text shows, the translator successfully employs the principle of wholeness in the mental process. For example, all the individual scenery images that the translator produces are related to the central image which conveys the tone of depression, including the sky, the sea water, the waves, some isles and "my" action near the sea. In order to achieve this effect, when translating the general background, the translator employs many concrete adjectives and nouns instead of those implicit and vague ones in the source text to reveal the pressure of the storm. For instance, "蓝色浓得惊人" is translated into "ghastly dark blue", where "ghastly" implies an unpleasant atmosphere and manifests more explicit oppression of the storm than the source text. "喋喃的声韵" is translated into "a humming sound", revealing the disorderly uneasiness of the waves before the storm. What's more, when the author expresses his feelings of bleakly sadness with "一种淡白无味的凄凉的情趣", the translator doesn't directly translate "情趣" into "temperament and interest" or "flavor". Instead, he refers to the author's feelings in the image-G, making some adjustments and skillfully translating "情趣" into a general "scene". He transforms the emotion into an image that contains both atmosphere and emotion, leaving more room of imagination for target readers. In the translated text, individual scenery images and "my" action form an image-G consistent with that of the original text, reproducing the dreary atmosphere of the seashore before a storm and the tone of depression.

4.1.1.3 Change of part of speech

Apart from the techniques employed in word meaning,

CHAPTER FOUR
AN ANALYSIS OF LITERARY ESSAY TRANSLATION FROM THE PERSPECTIVE OF GESTALT

the translator sometimes changes part of speech of the words in order to make the atmosphere created by the image-G in the translated text consistent with that of the source text. Different gestalt principles can achieve this effect. The following example illustrates the function of the principle of similarity in this respect.

Example 3

ST:

巷,是城市建筑艺术中一篇飘逸恬静的散文,一幅古雅冲淡的图画。(Cited in Zhang Peiji, Vol I, 2007: 267)

TT:

The lane, in terms of the art of urban architecture, is like a piece of prose of gentle gracefulness or a painting of classic elegance and simplicity. (Zhang Peiji, Vol I, 2007:270)

The source text points out the characteristics of the lane with two metaphors in parallelism. It uses altogether four adjectives in eight Chinese characters to manifest the elegance and gracefulness of the lane, expressing its beauty generally. If translated all in adjectives in English, these adjectives may cause redundancy in describing the lane, which not only is contradictory with the simplicity of the lane but also may result in ill readability. Therefore, the translator applies the principle of similarity during mental operation, viewing the adjacent two adjectives as a group. Then he adopts a common approach in literary translation: transforming the two adjectives that modify the same image in Chinese into the form of "attribute plus abstract noun" in English. As a result, "飘逸恬静" is translated into "gentle gracefulness" and "古雅冲淡" is reproduced as "classic elegance and simplicity". Through such a change of part of speech in image reproduction, the translator not only avoids redundant use of adjectives but also highlights the main features of the lane in a concise and elegant way that is consistent with the atmosphere embedded in the image-G based on the source text.

4.1.2 Gestalt principles and aesthetic harmony of structure: C-E

The translator needs to recognize the underlying structure

of the source text and present it correspondently in the target text instead of delivering the surface structure. The accomplishment of such transformation requires the translator to construct a mental representation of the source text components where the image is of great importance. As a result, the linguistic structure constraints can be greatly reduced thanks to the tracing of the image. (Jiang, 2002) Chinese and English display great discrepancy in the arrangement sequence of subject, predicate, object, adverbial and so on in a sentence. Therefore, the positions of some components need changing in translation in order to effectively reproduce the images and maintain the leading role of the image-G and topic, reproducing the harmonious structure.

4.1.2.1 Image-G oriented phrasal restructuring

In Chinese literary essays, after pointing out the subject or central image, authors like to attach many descriptions about it in the following part. Although divided by many commas, they altogether form a very long sentence that depicts various aspects of this image. However, a sentence in English may not allow so many descriptive parts in the parallel structure. Therefore, phrasal restructuring is inevitable in C-E translation. With the employment of the principle of continuity, the central feature of the image-G can be emphasized through restructuring.

Example 4

ST:

它所有的丫枝，一律向上，而且紧紧靠拢，也像是加过人工似的，成为一束，绝不旁逸斜出。它的宽大的叶子也是片片向上，几乎没有斜生的，更不用说倒垂了……这是虽在北方风雪的压迫下却保持着倔强挺立的一种树！(Cited in Zhang Peiji, Vol I, 2007:151)

TT:

Their twigs, also like things artificially shaped, all reach out towards the sky and grow close together in a cluster without any sideway growth. Their leaves are broad and point upwards with very few slanting sideways, much less upside down … They stand erect and unbending in face of North China's violent wind and snow. (Zhang Peiji, Vol I, 2007: 154)

CHAPTER FOUR
AN ANALYSIS OF LITERARY ESSAY TRANSLATION FROM THE PERSPECTIVE OF GESTALT

The source text is excerpted from a famous essay that depicts an object and eulogizes its fine characteristics called *Tribute to the White Poplar*. In sketching the appearance of the white poplar, the source text focuses on the upward growth of its twigs and leaves with plenty of clauses as well as the rhetorical device of exaggeration to reflect such characteristics of its growth. The upward growth is the core of the image-G. In translation, the translator adopts the principle of continuity during the mental actualization of the white poplar, placing the exaggerated description in front and incorporating the direct description of the growing gesture together, continuously maintaining the central position of the upward growth. To be specific, "也像是加以人工似的" is translated into "also like things artificially shaped", following right after the subject as parenthesis. On the other hand, "一律向上""而且紧紧靠拢" in the source text that both express the growing action of the white poplar are combined together by the translator as "all reach out towards the sky and grow close together" and assume the focus of the whole sentence. Also, "成为一束" "绝不旁逸斜出" are incorporated as "in a cluster without any sideway growth", depicting the gesture of the white poplar's growth in a supporting position in the whole sentence. With these adjustments, the action and gesture of the twigs are clearly reproduced in a continuous whole without being interrupted by the exaggerated part in the translated text. The translator's rearrangement of phrases makes the sentence structure clear-cut, which is consistent with the straightness of the white poplar. Under the foreshadowing of not only the content but also the sentence structure, it is more understandable to comprehend the final direct eulogy to the white poplar.

Also, some restructurings result from the syntactic discrepancy between Chinese and English. Many writers put plenty of adjectives before an object to express its characteristics in Chinese, but English sentences are always end-weighted with the complex part at the end. Under such circumstances, figure-ground segregation enhances the concentration on the core parts of the image-G. See the following example.

CHAPTER FOUR
AN ANALYSIS OF LITERARY ESSAY TRANSLATION FROM THE PERSPECTIVE OF GESTALT

Example 5

ST:

不过,它确实太纤细了。你看,那白茸茸的像透明的薄纱的翅膀,两根黑色的须向前伸展着,两点黑漆似的眼睛,几乎像丝一样细的脚。(Cited in Zhang Peiji, Vol IV, 2007: 171)

TT:

It was very slim. Its gossamer-like wings were white, downy and transparent. Its two black feelers were stretched ahead. Its two eyes were pitch-black. Its legs were thin like thread. (Zhang Peiji, Vol IV, 2007:173)

The source text depicts a slim and fragile butterfly after it experiences a rain; it acts as the image-G. The characteristics of this butterfly lie in the features of its wings, eyes and legs as well as the slow action of its feelers, the four individual images constituting the image-G. In the source text, the descriptions of these images are all in phrases with "wings" "eyes" and "legs" at the end. However, the translator transforms all the four phrases into sentences because of their important functions in revealing the delicateness of the butterfly. What's more, the translator employs figure-ground segregation during the mental process, putting "wings" "eyes" and "legs" at the beginning of each image, followed by their features emerging as new information in order to focus on the features of the butterfly. For example, "那白茸茸的像透明的薄纱的翅膀" is translated into "Its gossamer-like wings were white, downy and transparent". The translation of phrases depicting the butterfly's eyes and legs follows the same pattern. Through such adjustments of restructuring, the translator stands out the features as the figure. Together with the description of the feelers' weak action, the translated text vividly reproduces the whole image of the butterfly and successfully emphasizes its feebleness based on the source text.

In order to represent the atmosphere of the image-G embedded in the long sentences of the source text more explicitly, some adjacent parts that depict the same image are combined together through the principle of proximity in C-E translation.

CHAPTER FOUR
AN ANALYSIS OF LITERARY ESSAY TRANSLATION FROM THE PERSPECTIVE OF GESTALT

Example 6

ST:

我喜欢在春风中踏过窄窄的山径,草莓像个精致的红灯笼,一路殷勤地张结着。我喜欢抬头看树梢尖尖的小芽儿,极嫩的黄绿色里透着一派天真的粉红。(Cited in Zhang Peiji, Vol III, 2007:241)

TT:

I love to saunter in the spring breeze on a narrow mountain path bedecked with strawberries growing graciously like delicate red lanterns. I love to look up at treetops to watch tiny buds with their tender yellowish green tinged with an artless pink. (Zhang Peiji, Vol III, 2007:244)

In the source text the author depicts the beautiful spring mountain scenery that he loves. Therefore the author's deep affection for happiness in life is embedded in the linguistic description of the individual images of strawberries and trees. The source text sketches the scene of vigorous plants growing along the mountain path in spring, including the short strawberries and tall trees with their vigor as the core of the image-G. The emergence of strawberries and the description of their posture are separated in two clauses in the source text. So does the portraying of the trees. However, in the translated text, the translator applies the principle of proximity to combine the neighboring parts together. The three adjacent parts of the first sentence is integrated into a coherent sentence without a comma as "I love to saunter in the spring breeze on a narrow mountain path bedecked with strawberries growing graciously like delicate red lanterns". Through appropriate restructuring, the translated text emphasizes the experience of walking on the path, strengthening the feeling of an accidental encounter with the lovely strawberries. The restructuring of the second sentence reaches the same effect. As a result, the idleness underlying these images can be conveyed more effectively. What's more, removing commas in the translated text can not only make the reproduction of a relatively independent image more coherently without interruption but also reflect the vitality of these plants in form. Altogether the atmosphere of the image-G generated from the source text is fully represented.

Sometimes the translator conducts phrasal restructuring

CHAPTER FOUR
AN ANALYSIS OF LITERARY ESSAY TRANSLATION FROM THE PERSPECTIVE OF GESTALT

because the neighboring two groups of images are similar in the structure but slightly different in content focus. In the translation of literary essays that introduce local customs and practices, the translator may employ the principle of similarity to align the slight difference and unify these two groups in the structure.

Example 7

ST:
　　你就看那蔬菜摊子吧。这里有各种不同的颜色：紫色的茄子、白色的萝卜、红色的西红柿、绿色的小白菜,纷然杂陈,交光互影。这里又有各种不同的线条：大冬瓜又圆又粗,豆荚又细又长,白菜的叶子又扁又宽。就这样,不同的颜色、不同的线条,紧密地摆在一起,于纷杂中见统一。(Cited in Zhang Peiji, Vol IV, 2007:152)

TT:

Take for example the vegetable stall with its display of colors: purple eggplants, white radishes, red tomatoes, greenish cabbages. It also displayed various shapes: <u>round clumsy wax gourds</u>, <u>long narrow bean pods</u>, <u>flat wide cabbage leaves</u>. Hence, different colors and lines merged into an organic whole showing diversity in unity. (Zhang Peiji, Vol IV, 2007:154)

The source text depicts various food of Chinese daily life in a plain and imaginative way, comprehensively describing the vegetable stall of its rich colors and different shapes resulted from tidy arrangements of abundant vegetables of different categories. It portrays two groups of vegetables in the sequence of colors and shapes, which are parallel in the position of leading both groups. Therefore, the translator employs the principle of similarity during the mental actualization of the individual image of each vegetable in both groups and forms the image-G. In the translation of vegetables manifesting their colors, he maintains the phrasal structure of "adjectives plus nouns" with the vegetables as the focus. However, he changes the phrasal pattern of "nouns plus adjectives" into its opposite when reproducing the shapes of the vegetables. As s result, "大冬瓜又圆又粗,豆荚又细又长,白菜的叶子又扁又宽" is translated into "round clumsy wax gourds, long narrow bean pods, flat wide cabbage leaves" in order to keep a similar phrasal pattern with the former group of vegetables. Such restructuring in image reproduction not only avoids complexity and disorder if rendered directly but also creates the simple pleasant atmosphere of the daily life that the source text intends to convey.

4.1.2.2 Topic pattern sentence progression

Topic is the core issue that people want to express or explain. It can be a real object or an abstract concept, supplemented by other depictions or comments about it. When scenes change with the motion of the author, topic maintenance plays an important role in reproducing the harmonious structure. The principle of continuity can also be combined with the underlying spatial order in the translation of such descriptive writing.

Example 8

ST:

不论什么时候,你向巷中踅去,都如宁静的黄昏,可以清晰地听到自己的足音。不高不矮的围墙挡在两边,斑斑驳驳的苔痕,墙上挂着一串串苍翠欲滴的藤萝,简直像古朴的屏风。墙里常是人家的竹园,修竹森森,天籁细细……(Cited in Zhang Peiji, Vol I, 2007: 267-268)

TT:

At any hour of day, you can even distinctly hear in the dusk-like quiet your own footsteps. On either side of the lane stand enclosing walls of medium height, which, moss-covered and hung with clusters of fresh green wisteria, look almost like screens of primitive simplicity. Inside the walls are residents' gardens with dense groves of tall bamboos as well as soft sounds of nature. (Zhang Peiji, Vol I, 2007: 271)

CHAPTER FOUR
AN ANALYSIS OF LITERARY ESSAY TRANSLATION FROM THE PERSPECTIVE OF GESTALT

The source text establishes the lane as its topic and employs the following two images of scenes on the walls and inside them to further convey its stillness. "趄去" describes the motion of walking into the lane, indicating that the following scenes may change as the author steps at different locations of the lane. This main action denotes the description in a spatial order, which is not so obvious in the source text. The starting part of the first scene depicts the characteristics of the wall, which seems not consistent in the structure with the second scene that begins with the location of the wall. However, the translator recognizes the spatial order underlying the two scenes and threads them with the principle of continuity through changing the position of "on either side of the lane". He firstly points out that the walls are "on either side of the lane" at the beginning of the first scene, ensuring its consistency in the structure with the second scene. What's more, walls on two sides shape the lane in between, making it reasonable that the depiction of the moss and green wisteria on the walls also expresses the simple and unsophisticated scene of the lane. Later, with the continuous walking and sight moving, the readers can find the bamboo groves inside the wall and hear their soft sounds caused by breeze as the author does, which facilitates the stillness of the lane. When the spatial order is explicitly manifested in the translated text through the principle of continuity, the connection between the two sentences can be more coherent and the image-G based on the source text is harmoniously actualized through the smooth image reproduction.

The topic pattern can also make the topic more explicit when combined with the principle of wholeness in translation.

Example 9

ST:

初冬的天,灰黯而且低垂,简直把人压得吁不出一口气。前天一场雪还给居民一些明朗,但雪后的景象可不堪了!峭寒的北风将屋檐瓦角的雪屑一起卷到空中,舞过一个圈子以后都极善选择向路人脖项里钻。街道为恶作剧的阳光弄成泥淖,残雪上面画着片片践踏的痕迹。(Cited in Zhang Peiji, Vol II, 2007:223)

CHAPTER FOUR
AN ANALYSIS OF LITERARY ESSAY TRANSLATION FROM THE PERSPECTIVE OF GESTALT

TT:

It was early winter. The gloomy and low sky made one feel suffocating. A fall of snow a couple of days before had brought to the city dwellers a touch of brightness, but now what an ugly scene reigned! The raw wind sent the snow on the tiles along the eaves whirling in the air in tiny bits and adroitly making its way down the necks of the pedestrians by way of their collars. The streets had become slushy by exposure to the prankish sun, and the thawing snow was dotted with traces of footsteps. (Zhang Peiji, Vol II, 2007: 225)

The source text is excerpted from the very beginning of *The Ancient City* where the author sketches the bleak winter scene of the city after disasters. Winter is the overall topic of the source text, indicating the function of the principle of wholeness. Accordingly, the translator transforms the first sentence of the source text into two independent sentences. The first sentence of the translated text outstands winter as the topic and explicitly introduces the season. The whole second sentence of the translated text describes the gloom and oppression of the winter, reproducing the depressed atmosphere of the image-G clearly. With the first two sentences pointing out the topic and its characteristic as a leading whole, the translator later focuses on the scene of the winter city covered with snow. The principle of wholeness and the topic pattern also influence the translator in depicting this scene in that he keeps the snow as the subject all the time. Snow is the core of the image-G, thus the maintenance of snow as the subject sustains the winter scene as the image-G. In order to manifest the ugly scene after several days of snow falling, the translator adopts a bird's view. Firstly he captures the snow bullying people with the help of the cold wind. Then he overviews the city streets stained with black footsteps on the thawing snow. The whole scene of dreary cold winter is vividly reproduced through the topic maintenance during sentence progression, creating the harmonious structure.

Sometimes the topic of the latter sentence is the consequent action of the topic of the former one, and they altogether form a topic chain. In translation, the topic more related to the author's feelings needs to be emphasized with the application of figure-ground segregation.

Example 10

ST:

去的尽管去了,来的尽管来着;去来的中间,又怎样地匆匆呢？早上我起来的时候,小屋里射进两三方斜斜的太阳。太阳他有脚啊,轻轻悄悄地挪移了;我也茫茫然跟着旋转。(Cited in Zhang Peiji, Vol I, 2007:55)

TT:

What is gone is gone, what is to come keeps coming. How swift is the transition in between! When I get up in the morning, the slanting sun casts two or three squarish patches of light into my small room. The sun has feet too, edging away softly and stealthily. And, without knowing it, I am already caught in its revolution. (Zhang Peiji, Vol I, 2007: 57)

The source text expresses the author's melancholy about the rapid elapse of time with the depiction of a scene in daily life that conveys time passing. Therefore, the author's feelings are the core of the image-G. In the source text, the author firstly expresses his sadness; then he depicts the moving of the sun and later he describes the consequent action and feelings. The sun's movement and the author's feelings interconnect with each other with the former influencing the latter. As new information, the author's feelings become the figure while the moving of the sun forms the ground. Therefore, "我也茫茫然跟着旋转" is translated into a more complex sentence "And, without knowing it, I am already caught in its revolution" instead of the direct translation "I followed its revolution vacantly". The translator adopts figure-ground segregation in the mental actualization of the image-G and emphasizes the author's helplessness when facing time elapse. What's more, translating this relatively independent sentence into three parts also keeps a consistent structure with that of the former one and creates smooth organization to maintain the lyric flow of this literary essay successfully.

4.1.3 Gestalt principles and the consistency of aesthetic experience: C-E

Jiang Qiuxia has explained in detail about the consistency of aesthetic experience in the text production. The reproduction of literary texts encompasses not only the transference of necessary linguistic components but also the construction of a consistent translated text both in logic and aesthetics. Consistency requires the text to be a coherent and harmonious configuration that moves along a certain flow and maintains a certain gestalt quality like mood, tone. (Jiang, 2002) According to this statement, the consistency of aesthetic experience between the source text and the translated text relies on the reproduction of gestalt qualities, namely the contour and the mood or tone created by image-G representation. Therefore, the evaluations of atmosphere reproduction and emotion conveyance are necessary.

4.1.3.1 Atmosphere reproduction

Apart from scenery writing analyzed above, atmosphere is given more play in narrative writing where the author's main purpose is to express his thoughts and feelings through atmosphere creation. Heterogeneous isomorphism performs a crucial function in this respect.

Example 11

ST:

我颤巍巍地涉水步行,忽然想起自己的年龄。小时候,总感到年龄属于七老八十的长辈们,与自己无关。我的祖父六十岁时早已蓄须,不免显得老态,那时我只有十岁。现在我年已八十,在浑浊的水中,有如滚滚浪潮中的一叶孤舟。我闪避汽车开过的泥水飞溅,艰难地过马路……(Cited in Zhang Peiji, Vol IV, 2007:229)

TT:

As I tottered through the water, I suddenly thought of my age. When I was a kid, I used to think that age had nothing to do with me and associated it instead only with my elders in their seventies or eighties. When I was ten, my grandpa, at sixty, looked quite old for his age because of the beard he

CHAPTER FOUR
AN ANALYSIS OF LITERARY ESSAY TRANSLATION FROM THE PERSPECTIVE OF GESTALT

> was wearing. Now, as an octogenarian, I was like a solitary small boat drifting at the mercy of a large flow of muddy water. I barely managed to cross the street, taking care to dodge the muddy water splashed over by cars. (Zhang Peiji, Vol IV, 2007:231)

The author records an event: walking along the poor road covered with heavy rain water in his eighties. In order to manifest the difficulty in this process, the author firstly describes his slow and hard stepping in the water, then he brings about the contrast impressions between the image of his grandpa when the author was ten and that of the author himself at present, and finally he returns to the action of dodging from the muddy water. Through the narration of the source text, the author creates the tough atmosphere of this task and reveals his realization of ageing rapidly in the thoughts in between. The translator reproduces this toughness perfectly even in form after the employment of heterogeneous isomorphism, incorporating the author's feelings in the artistic expressions of the image of his elderly grandpa and promoting readers to aesthetically experience the author's memory in their mind as the author does. To be specific, the leading action that implies the difficulty of walking is "totter", which means moving with weak unsteady steps and usually at a slow pace. In the transference of the image of his grandpa, "我的祖父六十岁时早已蓄须,不免显得老态,那时我只有十岁" is translated into four parts as "When I was ten, my grandpa, at sixty, looked quite old for his age because of the beard he was wearing", which reveals the unsteady flow of thoughts at an old age and is consistent in form with the action "totter". After obtaining the tough atmosphere embedded in the source text, the translator linguistically reproduces it in the target text. The simile "a solitary small boat drifting at the mercy of a large flow of muddy water" in the translated text vividly reproduces the image of an old man in the flood with a bird's view. Last but not least, the translator adopts figure-ground segregation, placing "I barely managed to cross the street" as the main clause to outstand its position as the figure and to emphasize the tough atmosphere more explicitly. With the mentioned restructurings in image reproduction, the translator successfully conveys the tough atmosphere of the image-G in the translated text.

Sometimes different translators acquire different degrees

CHAPTER FOUR
AN ANALYSIS OF LITERARY ESSAY TRANSLATION FROM THE PERSPECTIVE OF GESTALT

of the atmosphere of image-G embedded in the source text and consequently reproduce it in dissimilar degrees. The assessment of which one is more consistent with that of the source text also depends on their linguistic actualizations of this image-G after the employment of the gestalt principles. The following example illustrates the influence of the principle of wholeness.

Example 12

ST:
那里的风,差不多日日有的,呼呼作响,好像虎吼。屋宇虽系新建,构造却极粗率,风从门窗隙缝中来,分外尖削,把门缝窗隙厚厚地用纸糊了,橡缝中却仍有透入。(Cited in Zhang Peiji, Vol IV, 2007:1)

TT1:
The wind blew practically every day there, booming and roaring like a tiger. Though the buildings were new, they were crudely constructed and the draught that came through the cracks round the door and windows nearly cut you in two. After we

had pasted layers of paper over these cracks, the wind still came in through gaps around the rafters. (David Pollard, 2000:164)

TT2:

The wind blew almost every day, howling like a tiger's roaring. The new houses were of poor quality, with a biting wind coming in through every chink in the doors and windows. And our efforts to have all the cracks sealed with paper nevertheless failed to stop it from breaking into the house. (Zhang Peiji, Vol IV, 2007:3)

It is clear that the wind is the subject matter throughout the source text. The author firstly points out its frequency and blowing sound; then he describes its penetrating force through the slots of the doors and windows in detail, altogether creating the image-G of the windy White Horse Lake. However, the subject of the second sentence seems like "houses". Thus the principle of wholeness is very important in the maintenance of the subject matter. In Version One, the translator at first establishes the wind as the subject according

CHAPTER FOUR
AN ANALYSIS OF LITERARY ESSAY TRANSLATION FROM THE PERSPECTIVE OF GESTALT

to the source text, but the wind loses its dominant place later. The subject deviates in the second sentence from the central image wind to the buildings, describing a lot about them and adding an object "you" to reflect the strong force of the wind. The subject of the adverbial clause of the third sentence turns into "we", placing the action of us and the wind at a parallel position. The second and third sentences are almost direct translations of the source text, resulting in multi focuses and the deviation from the subject matter. Because of the emphasis on each part, the force of the wind is exaggerated and the windy atmosphere is much stronger than that of the source text, which is not so appropriate. Version Two properly applies the principle of wholeness during the mental actualization of the image-G, emphasizing the description of the wind. Apart from the first sentence that directly depicts the wind's frequent and strong blow, the second and third sentences further highlight the wind by putting it in the dominant place. For instance, "屋宇虽系新建,构造却极粗率,风从门窗隙缝中来,分外尖削" is translated into "The new houses were of poor quality, with a biting wind coming in through every chink in the doors and windows". Although the subject is the buildings, it is set at the start of the second sentence as old information and becomes the ground. In this situation, the wind following it becomes the new information and occupies the position of the figure. Such arrangements effectively strengthen the important place of the wind. Moreover, the underlying subject of the third sentence is "we" that is hard to adjust; therefore, the translator incorporates the two clauses of the source text into one sentence without commas to generally reflect the force of the wind without much description of the details. Version Two altogether represents the atmosphere conveyed by the strong wind successfully in that it adopts the principle of wholeness and maintains the wind as the subject matter all the time in image reproduction.

4.1.3.2 Emotion conveyance

Some writers describe concrete objects and eulogize their good characteristics. The writers' thoughts about philosophy of life and affection or admiration towards the objects are embedded in writing through rhetorical devices such as personification. The following example presents the contribution of the principle of proximity in enhancing the conveyance of the author's emotions in translation.

CHAPTER FOUR
AN ANALYSIS OF LITERARY ESSAY TRANSLATION FROM THE PERSPECTIVE OF GESTALT

Example 13

ST:

它为着向往阳光,为着达成它的生之意志,不管上面的石块如何重,石块与石块之间如何狭,它必定要曲曲折折地,但是顽强不屈地透到地面上来,它的根往土壤钻,它的芽往地面挺,这是一种不可抗的力,阻止它的石块,结果也被它掀翻,一粒种子的力量的大,如此如此。(Cited in Zhang Peiji, Vol I, 2007:186-187)

TT1:

In order to get the sunshine and grow, it will wind its way up, no matter how heavy the rocks above and how narrow the space between the rocks. Its roots will drill downward and its sprouts will shoot upward. This is an irresistible force. Any rock lying in its way will be upset. This, further, shows how powerful a seed can be. (Liu Shicong, 2002:157,159)

TT2:

Seeking sunlight and survival, the young plant will labor tenaciously through twists and turns to bring itself to the surface of the ground no matter how heavy the

117

rocks overhead may be or how narrow the opening between them. While striking its roots deep into the soil, the young plant pushes its new shoots above ground. The irresistible strength it can muster is such as to overturn any rock in its way. See, how powerful a seed can be! (Zhang Peiji, Vol I, 2007:188-189)

The source text expresses the author's admiration to the power of the seed through detailed description of its growth process. Employing personification, the author creates the growing image of the seed vividly and arouses the empathy of the readers easily. In order to reach the similar effects, both versions of the translated texts employ personification accordingly and adopt verbs in the present tense to reflect the power of the young grass. In the concrete description of the grass' actions, it is obvious that the translators of both versions imagine the growing posture of the plant in that they both incorporate certain adjacent parts of the source text into a group and transform the abundant individual images into several scenes. Version Two applies the principle of proximity during the mental actualization of the image-G more effectively, recognizes the underlying three relatively complete scenes and reproduces them in a more holistic way. In Version Two, the first scene manifests the young grass' tenacious and flexible growth under the oppression of the heavy rocks in a long sentence without a comma by integrating the six adjacent clauses of the source text. Such unification in form also corresponds to the tenacious posture of the plant's persistent growth even under great pressure. The incorporation of the next two clauses concentrates on the young grass itself, directly describing the growing image of its roots and shoots. What's more, the third scene connects the following three clauses, outstanding the young plant with the overturned rocks, stressing its strength in a smoother way than the separated presentations of the plant and the rock in Version One. These integrations emphasize the power of the seed in a coherent way, reflecting the author's admiration to the seed and thoughts about the strength of life.

  Letters are also filled with the authors' feelings. The following example is excerpted from a letter written in semi-classical Chinese because of the prevailing temporal style. Although such a wording style is hard to represent in English, the emotion conveyance is successfully achieved by the translator through the employment of the principle of closure.

Example 14

ST:

人到高年,愈加怀旧,如弟方便,余当束装就道,前往台北探望,并面聆诸长辈教益。"度尽劫波兄弟在,相逢一笑泯恩仇。"遥望南天,不禁神驰……(Cited in Zhang Peiji, Vol I, 2007:365)

TT:

The longing for old friends grows with age. If it suits your convenience, I will pack and go on a visit to Taibei to consult our elders. "For all the disasters the brotherhood has remained; a smile at meeting and enmity is banished." When I look south towards the distant horizon, my heart cannot help going out to my compatriots there. (Zhang Peiji, Vol I, 2007:369)

It is necessary to introduce the historical background of this letter in order to comprehend the feelings embedded. Liao

CHAPTER FOUR
AN ANALYSIS OF LITERARY ESSAY TRANSLATION FROM THE PERSPECTIVE OF GESTALT

Chengzhi wrote a letter to Chiang Ching-Kuo, trying to persuade him into a peace talk. Therefore, mutual emotions that shared by both parties are persuasive and crucial in translation. The selected example is at the end of the letter where the author expresses his eagerness to reunification intensively. He even adopts two couplets of a poem written by Lu Xun. The translator focuses on the emotions underlying the poem and translates "度尽劫波兄弟在,相逢一笑泯恩仇" into "For all the disasters the brotherhood has remained; a smile at meeting and enmity is banished" to express the author's emotions evidently. What's more, the principle of closure is employed in the translation of "不禁神驰". The translator completes this image by pointing out the object of this action and translates it into "my heart cannot help going out to my compatriots there". With "compatriots" added to the image, the author's emotions become distinctly touching and this arouses the empathy of the readers more easily.

4.2 Image Reproduction in E-C Literary Essay Translation

After the above analysis of the image reproduction in C-E literary essay translation according to the combined approach, image reproduction in E-C literary essay translation will be illustrated in the following sections at lexical, structural and aesthetic experience levels. The translators' techniques evaluated from the perspective of gestalt will be revealed in the subtitles as well. Although these techniques are similar to those in C-E literary essay translation, differences occur under some circumstances.

4.2.1 Gestalt principles and aesthetic selection of lexical items: E-C

The most evident difference between the techniques applied in C-E and E-C translation occurs in the selection of lexical items. Many translators prefer the employment of four-character modules when translating English literary essays into

Chinese, resulting in meaning extension and aesthetic enhancement.

4.2.1.1 Meaning extension in four-character modules

Four-character modules can be dated from classical Chinese. According to Mao Ronggui (2005), four-character modules contain the Chinese four-character idioms that have been long established and hard to change because they derive from ancient stories and tell the principles of life or the fixed wording norms of articles written in classical Chinese. They can also refer to the four-character phrases or patterns created by the writer in contemporary era. In translation, if a translator translates "the moon and the breeze" into "明月清风" in Chinese, it is counted as a four-character module. What's more, "明月清风" extends the moon to be bright and the breeze to be soft, resulting in a meaning extension and an increase of aesthetic enjoyment. Thus in the reproduction of an image translated from English to Chinese, it is more of meaning extension than just meaning completion. The following example demonstrates the employment of four-character modules that reaches this effect in applying the principle of closure.

Example 15

ST:

I was this morning to buy silk for a nightcap: immediately upon entering the mercer's shop, the master and his two men, with wigs plastered with powder, appeared to ask my commands. They were certainly the civilest people alive; if I but looked, they flew to the place where I cast my eye; every motion of mine sent them running round the whole shop for my satisfaction. (Cited in Gao Jian, 2008:353-354)

TT:

今天上午我为睡帽事曾去买绸:我刚刚踏进一家绸缎店门,已有<u>头戴假发上敷香粉</u>的一位店主和他的两名伙计迎了上来,<u>听候吩咐</u>,论到<u>礼貌周到</u>,确乎<u>世间少有</u>。我的眼才一望,他们已顺着我的目光,到了那里;我只要稍稍指这指那,他们已在整个店里<u>团团打转</u>,以迎合我的心意。(Gao Jian, 2008:356)

The source text presents the scene of "my" buying silk in a shop where the shop men are extremely shrewd and

CHAPTER FOUR
AN ANALYSIS OF LITERARY ESSAY TRANSLATION FROM THE PERSPECTIVE OF GESTALT

attentive. Their characteristics are embedded in their appearance and motion, forming the image-G of person depiction. In order to transfer this image-G as a whole completely, the translator applies the principle of closure to fully imagine the scene depicted by the source text and reproduces it with the help of four-character modules. For instance, "with wigs plastered with powder" is translated as "头戴假发上敷香粉", reproducing every detail of the shop men's ornamentation and vividly conveying their underlying shrewdness. When it comes to the translation of their actions, with "to ask my commands" translated as "听候吩咐", the translator describes the shop men as willing to do anything for "me", adding the enthusiastic and even the servile attitude of them and extending the meaning of the original image. What's more, "They were certainly the civilest people alive" is translated into "论到礼貌周到,确乎世间少有" as a whole after the translator's adoption of the principle of closure, enriching the meaning of "civil" to be "polite and hospitable". "世间少有" also maintains the exaggerated comment about the shop men of the source text. Finally, "running around" is translated into "团团打转", vividly reproducing the image of the shop men's busy gesture in serving "me" and reflectively extending the attentiveness of them.

Apart from narrative writing depicting people, four-character modules can produce more aesthetic enjoyment in literary essays that portray scenes. Four-character modules contain more meanings with fewer words. As a result, if they occupy a large proportion of a text, image incorporation is inevitable. In a translated text nearly dominated by four-character modules, it is difficult to maintain the consistency of the images' positions.

Example 16

ST:

　　Nothing can be more imposing than the magnificence of English park scenery. Vast lawns that extend like sheets of vivid green, with here and there clumps of gigantic trees heaping up rich piles of foliage; the solemn pomp of groves and woodland glades, with the deer trooping in silent herds across them … (Cited in Xia Ji'an, 2000:74)

CHAPTER FOUR
AN ANALYSIS OF LITERARY ESSAY TRANSLATION FROM THE PERSPECTIVE OF GESTALT

TT1:

英国园林景致的妍丽确实天下无双。那里真的是处处<u>芳草连天</u>,<u>翠茵匝地</u>,其间<u>巨树蓊郁</u>,<u>浓荫翳日</u>;在那林薮与空旷处,不时可以瞥见结队漫游的鹿群……
(Gao Jian, 2008:305)

TT2:

英国公园的景色,最为宏伟,其壮观恐举世无出其右者。草地广阔,好像地上铺了鲜艳的绿色的毛毯;巨木数株,聚成一簇,<u>绿叶浓密</u>,一眼望去,草地上东一簇西一簇这一类的大树有不少;<u>矮树成林</u>,望之蔚然而<u>气象庄严</u>,林间空地之上,<u>麋鹿成群</u>,静静的走过……
(Xia Ji'an, 2000:75)

The source text creates the grand English park scenery with detailed descriptions of different images in the park, from the lawns, trees and groves to the deer among them. The lexical items in the source text are exquisite; therefore both translated versions employ four-character modules to enhance it. However, the atmospheres created by Version One and Version Two are different due to their respective selections of lexical items. In Version One, "magnificence" is recognized as "妍丽", which means beauty only. It loses the grandness of this scenery that is kernel in the source text, resulting in improper employment of gestalt principles in the detailed portraying of the scenery. In order to manifest "beauty" in form, the translator adopts the principle of simplicity to simplify the grandness that the source text emphasizes and to highlight beauty as the prevailing characteristic. The principle of simplicity is that the visual faculties focus on the most orderly and symmetric perception accordant with sensuous information. When the stimulus is vague, the perception is likely to be simple and regular as the "prevailing conditions" permit. "Prevailing conditions" mean the information logged by the primary visual faculty like retina (Rock & Palmer, 1990) Therefore, improper employment of this principle may lead to odd emphasis on the first impression and result in the implicit expressions of important details. Version One omits the simile of the lawns' extension and concludes them as "芳草连天,翠茵匝地", which means the beautiful extension of the green lawns to the horizon. It stresses the lawns' graceful beauty and causes the implicit expression of their wide grandness. Translating "with here and there clumps of gigantic trees heaping up rich piles of foliage" into "其间巨树

CHAPTER FOUR
AN ANALYSIS OF LITERARY ESSAY TRANSLATION FROM THE PERSPECTIVE OF GESTALT

蓊郁,浓荫翳日" also reveals the density of the tall trees in an implicit way. Altogether, the translator concentrates on the beauty of the English park scenery and incorporates the grandness of plants as decoration to the beauty, which doesn't fully reproduce the "magnificence" of the image-G.

Version Two, on the other hand, captures the magnificence of the English park scenery and manifests it in the detailed portraying of the plants and animals. With the employment of the principle of closure during the mental process and four-character modules in linguistic expressions, the translator even extends the connotations of images in the detailed scenes. For instance, "rich piles of foliage" is translated into "绿叶浓密", which not only reproduces the abundant amount of the tree leaves but also embodies their color as green. With "pomp of groves" translated into "矮树成林" and "solemn" translated into "气象庄严", the translator adds action and vigor to the groves and highlights the grandness of their clustering. It reaches the same effect in translating "the deer trooping in silent herds across them" into "麋鹿成群,静静的(地)走过". The four-character modules in Version Two altogether emphasize the meaningful details and strengthen the grandness of images in English park scenery through meaning extension.

4.2.1.2 Meaning adjustment

When translating certain culturally-loaded words that are not familiar to the target readers of the translated texts, meaning adjustments are necessary after the translator's employment of the principle of closure. Take another excerpt of E-C literary essay translation as an example.

Example 17

ST

We walked in so pure and <u>bright</u> a light, gilding the withered grass and leaves, so softly and serenely <u>bright</u>, thought I had never bathed in such a golden flood, without a ripple or a murmur to it. The west side of every wood and rising ground gleamed like a boundary of <u>Elysium</u> ... (Cited in Gao Jian, 2008: 262)

TT

我们漫步于其中的光照,是这样的纯美与熠耀,满目衰草木叶,一片金黄,晃晃之中又是这般柔和恬静,

CHAPTER FOUR
AN ANALYSIS OF LITERARY ESSAY TRANSLATION FROM THE PERSPECTIVE OF GESTALT

> 没有一丝涟漪,一息咽鸣。我想我从来不曾沐浴于这么幽美的金色光汛之中。西望林薮丘岗之际,彩焕烂然,恍若仙境边陲一般……(Gao Jian, 2008:263)

The author of the source text is Thoreau, who advocates simple life in nature and has written plenty of literary essays to depict and eulogize nature including the famous *Walden*. In this excerpt, Thoreau also depicts the sunset scene like a painting with the sunlight as the core of the image-G and manifests its brightness and softness. When depicting the scene of the light gleaming on the west wood, the author compares it to "boundary of Elysium" to express the magnificence and beauty of the sunset light. "Elysium" means "land of happiness" in Greek mythology, which is not familiar to Chinese readers. Therefore, the translator employs the principle of closure during the mental process and explains its meaning in Chinese as "仙境" on the whole, concisely making it explicit and leaving room of imagination for Chinese readers. As a result, it evidently reproduces the grandness of the sunset scene and the author's enjoyment of it. Among the abundant adjectives that directly describe the light, "bright" is used twice but the translator translates it differently. After applying the principle of wholeness, the first "bright" is translated into "熠耀", vividly reproducing the author's first impression of the fervent side of the light. The second "bright" is translated into "晃晃", which is much milder because the author also describes the soft side of the light. As a result, the magnificent sunset scene is reproduced with the manifestation of its brightness and softness. Altogether, the grand beauty and mild peace of the sunset image is successfully reproduced in the translated text.

4.2.1.3 Change of part of speech

Some lexical items appear to occupy the supporting position on surface structure in the source text, but they are kernel to the image presentation. The translator needs to stress them in the translated text through employing figure-ground segregation.

CHAPTER FOUR
AN ANALYSIS OF LITERARY ESSAY TRANSLATION FROM THE PERSPECTIVE OF GESTALT

Example 18

ST:

We walked in so pure and bright a light, gilding the withered grass and leaves, so <u>softly and serenely</u> bright, thought I had never bathed in such a golden flood, without a ripple or a murmur to it. (Cited in Gao Jian, 2008:262)

TT:

我们漫步于其中的光照,是这样的纯美与熠耀,满目衰草木叶,一片金黄,晃晃之中又是这般<u>柔和恬静</u>,没有一丝涟漪,一息咽鸣。我想我从来不曾沐浴于这么幽美的金色光汛之中。(Gao Jian, 2008:263)

The author describes both the dazzling side and the soft side of the light. Therefore "softly" and "serenely" stand out as the figure in conveying the mild characteristic of the light. The translator employs figure-ground segregation accordingly, translating them into "柔和恬静" and turning them from the decoration of "bright" into another main feature of the light. With appropriate employment of gestalt principles in the mental process and the change of part of speech in linguistic expressions according to the overall atmosphere embedded in the image-G generated from the source text, the translation of these words smoothly reveals the two sides of the light: brightness and softness.

4.2.2 Gestalt principles and aesthetic harmony of structure: E-C

As the same with the analysis of image reproduction in C-E literary essay translation on structure, image reproduction of E-C one will also be carried out at the phrasal and sentential levels following image-G oriented phrasal restructuring and topic pattern sentence progression.

4.2.2.1 Image-G oriented phrasal restructuring

The important function of image-G is mainly manifested in restructuring. "That is, when an image-G is mentally actualized and the linguistic actualization in the T-text is based on this image-G, a natural and consistent image will be produced, not restricted by the S-text structure." (Jiang, 2002: 144-145) As is mentioned in the former section,

CHAPTER FOUR
AN ANALYSIS OF LITERARY ESSAY TRANSLATION FROM THE PERSPECTIVE OF GESTALT

images in English literary essays are always articulated in long complex sentences. This section focuses on image reproduction internally embedded in the phrases in one sentence. The principle of wholeness is first of all employed in this respect.

Example 19

ST:

In this glade covered with bushes of a year's growth, see how the silvery dust lies on every seared leaf and twig, deposited in such infinite and luxurious forms as by their very variety atone for the absence of color. (Cited in Xia Ji'an, 2000:404,406)

TT:

森林里的空地上,长满已有一年左右历史的灌木;叶都焦了,枝就枯了,但请看树上的雪多么美丽!雪像银粉似地堆在上面,姿态万千,形状无穷;冬天是看不见色彩的,但是银珠玉叶无穷的形态似乎正可以补救色彩的缺乏。(Xia Ji'an, 2000:405,407)

This example is constituted by only one sentence, but it contains various individual images from the "glade" "bushes" "silvery dust" to the "leaf and twig". It is obvious that the "silvery dust" is different from the other three, outstanding as the core of the image-G. Therefore the translator rearranges the sequence of these images in the translated text and results in phrasal restructuring. Applying the principle of wholeness, the translator transforms this text into four parts after mentally picturing the component images into a whole scene. "In this glade covered with bushes of a year's growth" is translated into "森林里的空地上,长满已有一年左右历史的灌木" as the general background. With "seared leaf and twig" placed at the beginning of the second part as the ground, the translated version highlights the beautiful "silvery dust" and points it out as "雪" in order to make it more understandable. The most extraordinary restructuring occurs when the translator demonstrates clearly the complex object of the third clause of the source text and explains its supplementary parts in detail. The object which is "deposited" is the "silvery dust lies on every seared leaf and twig". What's more, because the "silvery dust" is the core of the image-G, the original supporting parts that supplement the features of it are emphasized, with "by their very

CHAPTER FOUR
AN ANALYSIS OF LITERARY ESSAY TRANSLATION FROM THE PERSPECTIVE OF GESTALT

variety atone for the absence of color" translated into "冬天是看不见色彩的,但是银珠玉叶无穷的形态似乎正可以补救色彩的缺乏". These restructurings in image reproduction together reveal the beauty and variety of the snow in detail with a clear scene presentation.

The above example illustrates several common adjustments according to the image-G based on the source text, but under certain circumstances, some parts need to be reversed in the translated text in order to highlight the core of the image-G after the employment of figure-ground segregation and the principle of closure.

Example 20

ST:

Opening the gate, we tread briskly along the lone country road, crunching the dry and crisped snow under our feet, or aroused by the sharp, clear creak of the wood sled, just starting for the distant market, from the early farmer's door, where it has lain the summer long, dreaming amid the chips and stubble ...
(Cited in Xia Ji'an, 2000:398)

TT:

把院子门打开,我们以轻快的脚步,跨上寂寞的乡村公路,雪干而脆,脚踏上去发出破碎的声音;早起的农夫,驾着雪橇,到远处的市场去赶早市。这辆雪橇一夏天都在农夫的门口闲放着,与木屑稻梗为伍,现在可有了用武之地。它的尖锐、清晰、刺耳的声音,对于早起赶路的人,也有提神醒脑的作用。(Xia Ji'an, 2000:399)

The source text adopts the view of "us" and creates the awakening scene of things related to the old-style production and life in a winter morning. It firstly depicts the image of "us" treading along the country road covered with snow; later it portrays the influence of the sound of the wood sled on "us" with "us" as the underlying object. "We" exist throughout the text by active action of "tread" and passive action of "aroused". As is shown in the translated text, "tread" is translated into "跨上" which is consistent with the source text at the starting part, but "aroused" is placed at the very end, translated as "也有提神醒脑的作用". Instead, the description of the wood sled appears at the beginning of the

CHAPTER FOUR
AN ANALYSIS OF LITERARY ESSAY TRANSLATION FROM THE PERSPECTIVE OF GESTALT

second part. The translator employs figure-ground segregation to conduct such a structural reversion because the focus of the second part is the wood sled, which interrelates with more other images, functions more effectively in constructing the environment and becomes the core of the image-G. Apart from this general reversion, the translator also restructures the detailed description of the wood sled through the application of the principle of closure. To be specific, "the wood sled, just starting for the distant market, from the early farmer's door, where it has lain the summer long, dreaming amid the chips and stubble" is translated into "早起的农夫,驾着雪橇,到远处的市场去赶早市。这辆雪橇一夏天都在农夫的门口闲放着,与木屑稻梗为伍". Through adding the farmer into this scene, the image of the wood sled becomes complete and reasonable. What's more, with the added farmer as the subject of the former half part, it is consistent with the sight of "us" at the beginning. The mentioned restructurings together reproduce the whole image, namely the awakening of an old-style simple life on a winter morning in harmonious structure.

4.2.2.2 Topic pattern sentence progression

In a text containing abundant images, a topic is essential to the harmonious arrangements of them, especially in English literary essays where these images are always separated in long complex sentences. The principle of continuity facilitates the translator to recognize the coherent characteristics of the image-G in the progression of individual images; figure-ground segregation enhances the translator to express these characteristics more explicitly.

Example 21

ST:

The shy king-fisher flew from the withered branch close at hand to another at a distance, uttering a shrill cry of anger or alarm. Ducks that had been floating there since the preceding eve were startled at our approach, and skimmed along the glassy river, breaking its dark surface with a bright streak. The pickerel leaped from among the lily-pads. The turtle, sunning itself upon a rock or at the root of a tree, slid

CHAPTER FOUR
AN ANALYSIS OF LITERARY ESSAY TRANSLATION FROM THE PERSPECTIVE OF GESTALT

suddenly into the water with a plunge. The painted Indian who paddled his canoe along the Assabeth three hundred years ago could hardly have seen a wilder gentleness displayed upon its banks and reflected in its bosom than we did. (Cited in Xia Ji'an, 2000:230,232)

TT1:

突然一只羞涩的翠鸟从附近一个枯枝上飞到远处,飞时发出一声尖叫,不知是惊是怒。在这里已经逗留隔宿的野鸭见到我们也猛然受惊,当它拂掠过晶莹的水面时,在那里掀起了一道道的白条。这里莲叶田田,叶间时有鱼跃。刚刚蹲在岸边的树根石上悠闲曝背的乌龟也突然一跃,潜入水中。此地的风物粗犷之中,饶具秀媚,假如一个文身涂面的印第安人三百年前曾泛舟这个溪上,他在波心岸边所见到的景色大概和我们也没有多大差异。(Gao Jian, 2008:285)

TT2:

羞涩的翠鸟,从附近的一根枯枝飞到远处的另一根枯枝,尖声发叫,不知是对我们这两个不速之客表示愤怒呢,还是惊惶。从昨夜起就在水上随意游行的鸭群,看见我们的船到,也受了惊吓,在波平如镜的水面

> 上一掠而过,暗绿的水面上,顿时划出一条明亮的白线。长满睡莲的浮叶丛中,忽然有小狗鱼跃出水面。在顽石上或树根上晒太阳的乌龟,泼剌一声滑到水里去了。这里的风景是荒野中带着静趣,想当年勾着花脸的印第安人,在亚莎白溪上驾着独木小舟,所能见到的溪畔风景或者是溪中反映出来的水光天色,也不过如此,三百年来竟没有什么改变。(Xia Ji'an, 2000: 231, 233)

The topic of the source text is the scenery along the Assabeth. With the specific depictions of four animals' movements in the scene along the brook, the writer comments on the characteristic of the scenery in the end as "wild gentleness". The two translated versions both successfully recognize this characteristic, translating it into "粗犷之中,饶具秀媚" or "荒野中带着静趣". They all emphasize the gentle enjoyment apart from the wildness along the brook. Under the direction of this topic, the joy triggered by the movements of animals is outstanding in both versions. The four individual images of animals' actions are consecutively revealed with the marching of "our" boat in the source text, so both versions adopt the principle of continuity and reproduce them one by one as in four independent sentences. The sentence progression forms harmonious structure as the source text does. However, the translations of the topic sentence are slightly different in two versions. It is a long complex sentence without a comma in the source text. Version One employs long complex phrases after pointing out the brook's characteristics, dividing the embedded images into inappropriate groups. Version Two points out each individual image and properly applies figure-ground segregation. It sets "the painted Indian" as the main character and "paddled his canoe along the Assabeth" as his movement with these two images together forming the ground. It later establishes the sighted scene of the brook as the figure and focuses on the everlasting wild gentleness of it without deviating to other subjects like "us". Through such restructuring in the image reproduction, the "wild gentleness" of the image-G is successfully conveyed.

4.2.3 Gestalt principles and the consistency of aesthetic experience: E-C

This section encompasses not only the atmosphere and emotion that are pointed out by Jiang Qiuxia as the major aesthetic qualities of an image-G, but also the wording style of the whole text in the image reproduction resulted from the image-G.

4.2.3.1 Atmosphere reproduction

As one of the gestalt qualities of an image-G, the atmosphere is the overall aura configured from the linguistic expression of the author's thoughts and feelings and occupies the dominant position on the reader's impression of the text. Consequently, heterogeneous isomorphism plays an important role in the atmosphere reproduction.

CHAPTER FOUR
AN ANALYSIS OF LITERARY ESSAY TRANSLATION FROM THE PERSPECTIVE OF GESTALT

Example 22

ST:

On one of those sober and rather melancholy days, in the latter part of Autumn, when the shadows of morning and evening almost mingle together, and throw a gloom over the decline of the year, I passed several hours in rambling about Westminster Abbey. There was something congenial to the season in the mournful magnificence of the old pile; and, as I passed its threshold, it seemed like stepping back into the regions of antiquity, and losing myself among the shades of former ages. (Cited in Xia Ji'an, 2000: 90)

TT:

时方晚秋,气象肃穆,略带忧郁,早晨的阴影和黄昏的阴影,几乎连接在一起,不可分别,岁云将暮,终日昏暗,我就在这么一天,到西敏大寺去信步走了几个钟头。古寺巍巍,森森然似有鬼气,和阴沉沉的季候正好相符;我跨进大门,觉得自己好像已经置身远古世界,忘形于昔日的憧憧鬼影之中了。(Xia Ji'an, 2000:91)

The source text is extracted from the very beginning of Irving's *Westminster Abbey* where the author firstly describes the seasonal environment as "melancholy" and later presents the abbey as "congenial to the season" and "mournful". Moreover, the author points out that "I lost myself among the shades of former ages", which reveals the haunting power of the dead. With the help of these adjectives and the description of "my" state, the author produces a dim and ghostly atmosphere. As is demonstrated in the translated text, it perfectly reproduces this atmosphere through appropriate diction. The translator applies heterogeneous isomorphism, absorbing the gloomy atmosphere and melancholy mood of the source text properly, reproducing them in the artistic expressions of individual images and triggering the reader's experience of the whole environment. For example, "sober" "melancholy" and "gloom" are translated into four-character modules "气象肃穆" "略带忧郁" and "终日昏暗", strengthening the single word's function of the source text in the creation of gloomy atmosphere. What's more, "in the latter part of Autumn" and "the decline of the year" are translated into "时方晚秋" and "岁云将暮", forming a parallelism with the words that directly describe the atmosphere and increasing their expressive effect more smoothly. Last but not least, the ghostly atmosphere is modestly embedded in the image-G based on the original text as "mournful magnificence", but the haunting power is strong enough to make "me" "lost myself". Therefore, the translator translates "the shades of former ages" into "昔日的憧憧鬼影" and "mournful magnificence" into "古寺巍巍,森森然似有鬼气" to reproduce such an atmosphere explicitly. The translator's reproduction of the images of the seasonal environment and "my" being lost in the dead men's shades both represent the atmosphere of the source text successfully.

4.2.3.2 Emotion conveyance

Emotion is the other gestalt quality proposed by Jiang Qiuxia as the mood or tone, which is especially important in literary essays where the author expresses affection or other feelings towards an object or a person. Several gestalt principles can achieve this effect. The following translation of a lyric text demonstrates the combination of the principles of proximity and similarity.

Example 23

ST:

She felt happy and good, like a child in an orchard, ripe apples and pears tumbling in soft grass about her, the silver boat of the moon riding in a green sky. For her birds sang, sweet bells chimed and clashed, the stars made a queer, thin, tinkling song on still and moonless nights … (Cited in Gao Jian, 2008:19-20)

TT:

她幸福和快活得像果园中的儿童似的,周围的软草上滚动着熟了的苹果和梨子,碧绿的天空上荡漾着银白的新月之舟。为了她,禽鸟在歌唱,悠扬的钟声在嗡鸣回荡,天边的群星在静寂无月的夜晚在奏唱着一曲曲奇异幽细的丁冬之歌……(Gao Jian, 2008:22)

The original text narrates the life and happiness of her with the description of beautiful things surrounding her to reflect her happiness. The author's affection towards her is obvious through the creation of five images of beautiful

CHAPTER FOUR
AN ANALYSIS OF LITERARY ESSAY TRANSLATION FROM THE PERSPECTIVE OF GESTALT

things. The image of apples and pears and that of the moon is presented in the parallel structure at the supplementary position in the source text, but the details in them are significant to reflect her happiness. Therefore, the translator applies the principle of similarity and transforms them into two relatively independent clauses. The latter three images are scattered too much by commas in the source text, but the translator employs the principles of proximity and similarity properly to recognize which words stand closer and fall into a similar domain, describing the same image. What's more, with "riding" translated into "荡漾", "the silver boat of the moon" translated into "银白的新月之舟" and "a queer, thin, tinkling song" translated into "一曲曲奇异幽细的丁冬之歌", the aesthetic lexical selections also reveal the author's affection. Altogether, the emotional orientation of the five images in the translated text is consistent with that embedded in the image-G based on the source text.

Sometimes the translator makes adjustments of the sentence type based on the image transference in order to ensure the consistency of tones between the source text and the translated text. The following example illustrates the application of the principle of closure in achieving this effect.

Example 24

ST:

This rambling propensity strengthened with my years. Books of voyages and travels became my passion, and in devouring their contents I neglected the regular exercises of the school. How wistfully would I wander about the pier-heads in fine weather, and watch the parting ships, bound to distant climes. With what longing eyes would I gaze after their lessening sails, and waft myself in imagination to the ends of the earth. (Cited in Xia Ji'an, 2000:62)

TT1:

这种浪游的习性在我竟随着年齿而俱增。描写海与陆的游记成了我的酷嗜,寝馈其中,致废课业。我往往怀着多么渴慕的心情漫步在码头周围,凝视着一艘艘离去的船只驶赴迢递的远方;我曾以何等希羡的眼神目送着那渐渐消逝的桅帆,并在想象之中自己也随风飘越至地角天边!(Gao Jian, 2008:300)

CHAPTER FOUR
AN ANALYSIS OF LITERARY ESSAY TRANSLATION FROM THE PERSPECTIVE OF GESTALT

TT2:

岁月增添,游兴更盛。我最爱读的书是游记旅行之类,废寝忘餐读这种闲书,把学校里的正课练习都给耽误了。风和日暖之日,我到码头四周去游荡,看见船只一艘一艘的开向远方,不禁心向往之——船帆渐远渐小,岸上的我,以目远送,我的灵魂已经随着我的幻想到了地球的不知哪一个角落了。(Xia Ji'an, 2000: 63)

The original text expresses the author's affection and eagerness to ramble in a reminiscent tone. The two translated versions both adopt four-character modules and semi-classical Chinese to facilitate this tone. For instance, "and in devouring their contents I neglected the regular exercises of the school" is translated into "寝馈其中,致废课业" in Version One. In Version Two, "This rambling propensity strengthened with my years" is translated into "岁月增添,游兴更盛". However, evaluated from the perspective of image reproduction, Version Two presents a better performance. The source text recalls the scene of "my" watching the departing ships and the emotion of "my" eagerness to travel triggered by the ships. When translating this scene and feelings, Version One directly transplants the structure and word sequence of the source text, causing the deviation from the image and reduction of tone of reminiscence. On the other hand, Version Two applies the principle of closure to completely reproduce the image of "my" watching ships' departure and maintains the reminiscent tone of the source text from a comprehensive view. To be specific, the exclamation that the author releases upon seeing the ships going away is wholly integrated into a scene where the author's motion and sight form the majority of it and his feelings emerge naturally. The incorporation of the mood into an overall image works the same way in the translation of the last sentence. Four-character modules and semi-classical Chinese also enhance the tone of reminiscence. Altogether, Version Two conveys the emotion of the image-G more properly on the basis of image reproduction.

4.2.3.3 Consistency of wording style

Style in literary works has been defined by many scholars mainly from two aspects. Buffon puts forward that "Style is the man" and Schopenhauer proposes that "Style is the physiognomy of the mind" (Feng, 2002:106). They both

CHAPTER FOUR
AN ANALYSIS OF LITERARY ESSAY TRANSLATION FROM THE PERSPECTIVE OF GESTALT

claim that style reflects the personality and thoughts of the writer from the macro view. Chinese scholar Liu Zhongde concludes "style" not only from the macro view as the writer's thoughts, feelings and aesthetic accomplishments but also from the micro view as the organization of words, phrases, sentences and paragraphs. (1991: 122) According to the explanations about style above, it is obvious that the definition of style encompasses two aspects: the writer's thoughts or personality as well as the particular linguistic expressions. In fact, the former sections have discussed a lot about these two aspects, but the particular wording style needs to be emphasized in E-C literary essay translation. Since the selected English essays are mostly written in the nineteenth century, their wording is mainly of the antiquely refined style. Therefore, if they are translated into four-character modules or semi-classical Chinese, the wording style of the translated text can be consistent with that of the source text.

Example 25

ST:

The leafless trees become spires of flame in the sunset, with the blue cast for their background, and the stars of the dead calices of flowers, and every withered stem and stubble rimed with frost, contribute something to the mute music. (Cited in Gao Jian, 2008:266-267)

TT1:

绮照落辉之下,无数光净枝桠,背负东天穹苍,顿时幻作金阙玉宇,光焰烛天;而地面降英落花,璨若金盏,残根败株,缀满霜华,这一切都汇成一曲曲非人耳所能谛听到的无声妙籁。(Gao Jian, 2008:274)

TT2:

霞光照处,秃树皆熠熠如尖塔着火,东方一片蔚蓝,成为极妙的背景;花朵谢落,然花萼点点犹如繁星;败枝残干,风霜之迹斑斑——这一切都构成了我面前无声的音乐。(Xia Ji'an, 2000:165,167)

CHAPTER FOUR
AN ANALYSIS OF LITERARY ESSAY TRANSLATION FROM THE PERSPECTIVE OF GESTALT

The source text employs the rhetorical device of synaesthesia that connects the feelings of different sensory organs and realizes the transformation of feelings from one sense to another through imagination, enabling "me" to hear mute music from the extremely beautiful scene in front of "my" eyes. The images in the source text are exquisite, calling for the employment of four-character modules and semi-classical Chinese in translation. The two translated versions are both constituted by four-character modules in semi-classical Chinese with Version One reproducing the beauty of the image-G better. The source text contains three individual images, including the shiny leafless trees decorated by the sunset, the dead calices of flowers on the ground as well as their shriveled stem and stubble ornamented with frost on the edge. The translation of the first two images in two versions both maintains their beauty, with Version One adding more gorgeousness into the image-G. To be specific, "and the stars of the dead calices of flowers" is translated into "而地面降英落花,璨若金盏". However, Version Two embeds some inappropriate vicissitudes in the third image, translating "every withered stem and stubble rimed with frost" into "败枝残干,风霜之迹斑斑" with "斑斑" indicating something

155

ugly. On the other hand, Version One adopts the principle of similarity during the mental process, reproducing all three images in a similar complimentary tone and creating a splendid sunset scene. Tidy four-character modules in semi-classical Chinese of Version One also enhance the exquisite parallelism of the source text, remaining the aesthetic consistency of the antiquely refined wording style.

4.3 A Comparative Study of Image Reproduction in C-E and E-C Literary Essay Translation

In this section, a comprehensive comparison between the image reproduction in C-E and E-C literary essay translation will be conducted at three levels according to the combined approach. The similarities and differences will be illustrated in the following two tables (Table 4.1 and Table 4.2) in terms of the employment of gestalt principles as well as the techniques that translators adopted in linguistic expressions. Similarities in these two aspects are in bold type.

Table 4.1 The employment of gestalt principles in C-E and E-C literary essay translation

	Lexical level	Structural level	Aesthetic experience level
C-E	Principle of closure Principle of wholeness Principle of similarity	Principle of continuity Figure-ground segregation Principle of proximity Principle of similarity **Principle of wholeness**	**Heterogeneous isomorphism** Figure-ground segregation Principle of wholeness **Principle of proximity** Principle of closure
E-C	Principle of closure Principle of wholeness Figure-ground segregation	**Principle of wholeness** Principle of closure **Principle of continuity** **Figure-ground segregation**	**Heterogeneous isomorphism** Principle of similarity **Principle of proximity** Principle of closure

Table 4.2 Translator's techniques in linguistic expressions in C-E and E-C literary essay translation

	Lexical level	Structural level	Aesthetic experience level
C-E	Meaning completion Meaning adjustment Change of part of speech	Image-G oriented phrasal restructuring Topic pattern sentence progression	Atmosphere reproduction Emotion conveyance
E-C	Meaning extension Meaning adjustment Change of part of speech	Image-G oriented phrasal restructuring Topic pattern sentence progression	Atmosphere reproduction Emotion conveyance Consistency of wording style

4.3.1 Lexical level

The comparison between C-E and E-C literary essay translation at the lexical level from the perspective of gestalt focuses on the selection of lexical items after the translator's referring to the whole context. Therefore, at the lexical level, the present study emphasizes the whole restricting the parts both in the meaning and the form of lexical items.

In terms of the similarities, the principle of closure

CHAPTER FOUR
AN ANALYSIS OF LITERARY ESSAY TRANSLATION FROM THE PERSPECTIVE OF GESTALT

assumes the dominant place in identifying the meanings of lexical items in both C-E and E-C literary essay translation. This is because literary essays support the author to express his thoughts and feelings in a direct way. If an indeterminate spot or blankness occurs, the translators of both C-E and E-C translation tend to complete it. For example, "潭柘寺的钟声" is translated into "Tan Zhe Si with its reverberating bell" with the added "reverberating" to complete the image. And "the civilest people" is translated into "礼貌周到,世间少有" to specify that their civilization lies in being polite and to suit the overall atmosphere of the event. The principle of wholeness is also shared by C-E and E-C literary essay translation in meaning adjustment. To be specific, "情趣" is translated into "scene" because after reading the former parts that depict the bleak environment, the translator understands that the author's depressed emotion arises from the whole scene. The second "bright" is translated as "晃晃", adjusting the meaning to reveal the mild side of the light after referring to the overall atmosphere. Another similarity is that both C-E and E-C translation support the change of part of speech of lexical items in form, but such changes arise from different applications of gestalt principles in C-E and E-C literary essay translation. It will be illustrated in the following part.

Differences between C-E and E-C literary essay translation are huger than the similarities in the selection of lexical items. To begin with, although they both adopt the principle of closure to identify the meaning and complete the image, this principle results into more meaning extension than just meaning completion in E-C translation because of the employment of four-character modules. For instance, "pomp of groves" is translated into "矮树成林", which not only reproduces the grandness of the groves concretely but also adds vigor into the groves through the motion "成". In addition, the changes of part of speech in C-E and E-C translation result from different applications of gestalt principles. For example, "古雅冲淡" is translated into "classic elegance and simplicity" after the translator applying the principle of similarity. The original words are both adjectives which are grouped together, and the form of "adjective plus noun" can avoid the ill readability resulted from the frequent use of adjectives and remain the clear gracefulness of the lane in form. In E-C translation, "softly and serenely" is translated into "柔和恬静" for the application of figure-ground segregation to highlight the equivalent important gentle side of the light and better manifest the characteristics of the image-G through the successful image reproduction.

4.3.2 Structural level

The comparison of the image reproduction between C-E and E-C literary essay translation at the structural level is conducted on phrases and sentences. Summarizing the analyses above, it is clear that C-E and E-C literary essay translation share more similarities in sentence progression and display more discrepancy in phrasal restructuring.

In terms of similarities, the underlying gestalt principles shared by C-E and E-C literary essay translation are the principle of wholeness, the principle of continuity and figure-ground segregation. The application of the principle of wholeness often results in more fluent word groups. For instance, "初冬的天,灰黯而且低垂,简直把人压得呀不出一口气" is translated into "It was early winter. The gloomy and low sky made one feel suffocating" as two independent sentences with the first sentence clearly pointing out the topic. In E-C translation, as Example 19 demonstrates, the principle of wholeness supports the translator to restructure one sentence in English into four relatively independent parts in Chinese in order to reproduce the image of twigs covered by snow in a more fluent and natural expression. The employment of the principle of continuity often occurs in descriptive writings where the scenes change with the motion of the author. Since the topic and spatial order are clear in the source text, the translated text usually maintains the structure of the source after the translator's employing the principle of continuity. It is already exemplified with the Example 8 in C-E translation and Example 21 in E-C translation. Figure-ground segregation also plays an important role in the formation of the harmonious structure. In C-E translation, "我也茫茫然跟着旋转" is translated into "And, without knowing it, I am already caught in its revolution" in order to highlight "my" blank melancholy since such a feeling is the centre of the image-G. In E-C translation, as is illustrated by Example 21, Xia's translation of the last sentence stresses the everlasting scene along the brook as the salient figure without deviating to "us". Another similarity is that both C-E and E-C literary essay translation follow image-G oriented phrasal restructuring and topic pattern sentence progression.

The differences between C-E and E-C literary essay

CHAPTER FOUR
AN ANALYSIS OF LITERARY ESSAY TRANSLATION FROM THE PERSPECTIVE OF GESTALT

translation mainly rest on phrases. Although they both follow image-G oriented phrasal restructuring, the underlying gestalt principles vary one another. In C-E translation, Example 4 displays the translator's continuous concentration on the growing posture of the white poplar by putting "also like things artificially shaped" at the beginning part and later focusing on its upward growth to continuously maintain the image-G after applying the principle of continuity. In E-C translation, as Example 20 demonstrates, the depiction of the wood sled is completed in detail with the employment of the principle of closure while the action of us being "aroused" is reversed at the end of the translated text according to figure-ground segregation in order to better manifest the cold sober atmosphere of the image-G through the smooth image reproduction. The principle of proximity and the principle of similarity are also employed to form the harmonious structure in C-E translation as illustrated in Examples 6 and 7. Apart from the underlying gestalt principles, the transformations of linguistic expressions are also different in C-E and E-C translation. According to Wang Yin (1990: 24-40), the structure of English sentences is like that of grapes where diverse branches and fruits can derive from a short trunk;

while the structure of Chinese sentences is like that of bamboos constituted by the sequential stretch of phrases consecutively. Therefore, phrases are often incorporated in one long complex sentence in C-E translation. For example, "我喜欢在春风中踏过窄窄的山径,草莓像个精致的红灯笼,一路殷勤地张结着" is translated into "I love to saunter in the spring breeze on a narrow mountain path bedecked with strawberries growing graciously like delicate red lanterns" where "一路殷勤地张结着" is incorporated in the sentence as "bedecked ... growing graciously" in order to reappear the lightly cheerfulness of the image-G through the coherent reproductions of "my" walking and the appearance of strawberries. On the other hand, a long complex sentence is always translated into several phrases in E-C translation as is demonstrated in Example 19.

4.3.3 Aesthetic experience level

The comparison between C-E and E-C literary essay translation at the aesthetic experience level is mainly conducted on the evaluation of atmosphere reproduction and emotion conveyance, but E-C translation also achieves the consistency in wording style thanks to the employment of four-character modules and semi-classical Chinese.

Starting with the similarities between C-E and E-C literary essay translation, the present study finds that the underlying gestalt principles shared by both are heterogeneous isomorphism, the principle of proximity and the principle of closure. Heterogeneous isomorphism is essential in atmosphere reproduction. To be specific,"我的祖父六十岁时早已蓄须,不免显得老态,那时我只有十岁"is translated into "When I was ten, my grandpa, at sixty, looked quite old for his age because of the beard he was wearing" with plenty of commas to reproduce the unsteady and slow mental flow of an old man and embed the tough struggle of the author in the linguistic reproduction of the whole image. In Example 22, the gloomy and ghostly atmosphere of the Westminster Abbey is perfectly reproduced after the translator's application of heterogeneous isomorphism and aesthetic lexical selections. The principle of proximity helps the translator recognize a relatively independent image as a whole correctly when it is scattered by commas in form. For example,"这是一种不可抗的力,阻止它的石块,结果也被它掀翻"is incorporated in a sentence as "The irresistible strength it can muster is such as to overturn any rock in its way", which better represents the hidden strength of the seed. In E-C translation, "birds sang, sweet bells chimed and clashed, the stars made a queer, thin, tinkling song on still and moonless nights …" is properly recognized by the translator as three individual images with the help of the principle of proximity and the principle of similarity. The principle of closure facilitates the translator to strengthen the emotion and tone of the source text. In C-E translation, "不禁神驰" is translated into "my heart cannot help going out to my compatriots there" with "my compatriots" added to convey the author's emotion more sincerely. In E-C translation, the two exclamation sentences in Example 24 are translated into two images with emotions in order to enrich the image-G and maintain the reminiscent tone of the source text.

The most obvious difference between C-E and E-C translation at the aesthetic experience level lies in that E-C translation better retains the antiquely refined wording style of some English literary essays with the help of four-character modules and semi-classical Chinese wording. For instance, the excerpted text in Example 25 depicts an extremely beautiful scene of the nature decorated by sunset with exquisite words. The translator of Version One perfectly reproduces the beauty with concise four-character modules and semi-classical Chinese and even strengthens it with lexical items like "绮照落辉" that contain more aesthetic enjoyment. What's more, the underlying gestalt principles are also various at the aesthetic experience level. The principle of wholeness is essential in representing the image-G as an integrated whole through the proper image reproduction as illustrated in Example 12. The principle of similarity helps the translator reproduce a relatively independent image whose atmosphere and emotion are consistent with those of the image-G based on the source text as is illustrated in Example 25.

4.4 Summary

Through the analyses of both C-E and E-C literary essay translation above, the present study proves that gestalt principles and the theory of image-G actualization can be combined to research image reproduction in literary essay translation. With gestalt principles as the underlying motives and three aspects of the theory of image-G actualization as the evaluation levels, the present study finds that the principle of closure, the principle of wholeness, the principle of similarity and figure-ground segregation can be applied in the aesthetic selection of lexical items with the first one occupying the dominant place. When it comes to the formation of harmonious structure, the principle of wholeness, the principle of continuity, figure-ground segregation, the principle of proximity, the principle of similarity and the principle of closure can influence the translator's restructuring on the basis of the image-G. In addition, the first three principles are shared by both C-E and E-C translation. At the aesthetic experience level, heterogeneous isomorphism, the principle of proximity, the principle of closure, the principle of wholeness, the principle of similarity and figure-ground segregation facilitate the translator to reproduce the atmosphere and emotion of the source text. The first three principles are shared by C-E and E-C translation.

The present study finds that all seven gestalt principles can influence the translator in both C-E and E-C translation in terms of at least one of the three levels. What's more, the principle of closure is the most powerful one because literary essays express the author's thoughts and feelings freely through images. In order to explicitly convey this freedom to target

CHAPTER FOUR
AN ANALYSIS OF LITERARY ESSAY TRANSLATION FROM THE PERSPECTIVE OF GESTALT

readers, translators of both directions tend to complete the images and fully reveal their meanings and emotions through the principle of closure.

It also finds that the employment of four-character modules in E-C translation brings about many effects. They can not only extend the meaning and aesthetic enjoyment of the lexical items in the source texts but also maintain the antiquely refined wording style of the English essays in former times.

CHAPTER FIVE

CONCLUSION

CHAPTER FIVE
CONCLUSION

This chapter comes into the conclusion based on the former four chapters. Major findings and limitations of this research are demonstrated. It also provides suggestions for future study.

5.1 Major Findings

Literary essays have been recognized as "aesthetic writing" throughout the world all the time thanks to the rich images and feelings embedded in them. Therefore, this study firstly refers to the theory of image-G actualization that research images in literary works from the aesthetic perspective, advocating that literary translation requires not only the representation of linguistic meaning but also the conveyance of aesthetic value. The theory of image-G actualization draws from the law of prägnanz (mainly the principle of closure) of gestalt psychology as the foundation of its theoretical model, which inspires the present study to explore the possibility of other applications of gestalt principles in the research of image reproduction in literary essays. Altogether, the present study attempts to combine gestalt principles with the theory of image-G actualization to research image reproduction in both C-E and E-C literary essay translation from the perspective of gestalt. The major findings are as follows:

To begin with, it is feasible to combine gestalt principles with the theory of image-G actualization with the former serving as the underlying motives in the translator's mental actualization of images and image-G and the three aesthetic effects (i.e. lexical, structural and aesthetic experience) articulated from the image-G as the evaluation levels. Gestalt principles come into play at all three levels. The advantages of the combined approach lie in two aspects. On one hand, it reveals that gestalt principles are the theoretical motivation in the mental actualization of image-G, which clarifies the translator's mental process in detail. On the other hand, it

CHAPTER FIVE
CONCLUSION

proves that other six gestalt principles, besides the principle of closure, are also influential to image reproduction in literary essay translation. Altogether, the combined approach anchors on Jiang Qiuxia's theory of image-G actualization, employs gestalt principles to compensate for its blurred mental process and makes a relatively systematic approach.

Thanks to the applications of gestalt principles, the translated texts achieve aesthetic effects at three levels: the lexical level, the structural level and the aesthetic experience level. At the lexical level, since the gestalt perspective highlights the influence of the whole on parts and literary essays help the author express his feelings in a free way, the principle of closure becomes the most influential principle for the translator in selecting the most appropriate lexical items and even adding proper words to fill in the blankness in the source text, reproducing the images more explicitly and completely. The principle of wholeness also plays an important role in helping the translator choose suitable lexical items according to the atmosphere and emotion embedded in the image-G based on the source text. Other gestalt principles, such as the principle of similarity and figure-ground segregation, are helpful in determining an appropriate part of speech for the lexical items in the translated text in order to reproduce the characteristics of images equivalently and naturally. At the structural level, more gestalt principles serve to form the harmonious structure of the translated text. The principle of wholeness again helps the translator rearrange the surface structure of the source text in order to represent the gestalt qualities of the image-G in a natural and consistent way. The principle of continuity supports the translator to maintain the topic through restructuring and to ensure that all the reproductions of individual images are related to the image-G in a certain order. Figure-ground segregation enhances the focus on those images that are crucial to the reproduction of image-G through proper restructuring. Other gestalt principles, such as the principle of proximity, the principle of similarity and the principle of closure, are also advisable in recognizing a relatively independent image as a whole and reproducing it explicitly and completely. At the aesthetic experience level, heterogeneous isomorphism is the main principle in the atmosphere reproduction because it helps the translator absorb the emotion of the author and choose correspondent lexical items and structure to create an atmosphere indicating that emotion. The principle of proximity

CHAPTER FIVE
CONCLUSION

supports the translator to identify an overall image out of abundant commas and to reproduce its underlying emotion wholly. The principle of closure once again functions to complete the emotion of the source text and to convey the implicit mood more explicitly and thoroughly. Other principles, such as figure-ground segregation, the principle of wholeness and the principle of similarity, all promote the translator in conveying the emotions of the source text by the selection of lexical items containing correspondent emotions or restructuring to better manifest the overall image. Viewing from the detailed summary, it is obvious that one gestalt principle functions in terms of at least one level. Therefore, apart from the principle of closure, other six gestalt principles also lead to aesthetic effects in the image reproduction of literary essays.

The comparison between C-E and E-C literary essay translation is conducted on the applications of gestalt principles and linguistic techniques employed by the translators at three levels. In terms of the gestalt principles applied at the lexical level, the principle of closure and the principle of wholeness are employed in both C-E and E-C translation. C-E translation also adopts the principle of similarity. At the structural level, the principle of wholeness, the principle of continuity and figure-ground segregation are shared by C-E and E-C literary essay translation, with C-E translation additionally employing the principle of proximity and the principle of similarity while E-C translation applying the principle of closure. At the aesthetic experience level, heterogeneous isomorphism, the principle of proximity and the principle of closure are adopted by both C-E and E-C literary essay translation, but C-E translation employs extra figure-ground segregation and the principle of wholeness while E-C translation draws on the principle of similarity. When it comes to the specific techniques applied by the translators at the three levels, differences are huger than similarities in C-E and E-C translation. At the lexical level, although the translators from both directions conduct meaning completion, meaning adjustment and change of part of speech, meaning completion in E-C translation is more of meaning extension because of the employment of four-character modules. At the structural level, although translators of both C-E and E-C literary essay translation follow image-G oriented phrasal restructuring and topic pattern sentence progression, C-E translation tends to simplify the meanings of certain phrases into words embedded

CHAPTER FIVE
CONCLUSION

in a long sentence with modifiers while E-C translation often completes and extends the meanings of certain phrases and even transforms them into relatively independent sentences. At the aesthetic experience level, both C-E and E-C translators can achieve successful atmosphere reproduction and emotion conveyance of the image-G with the guidance of proper gestalt principles. E-C translation, in addition, can achieve extra consistency of wording style with the employment of four-character modules.

To sum up, gestalt principles and the theory of image-G actualization can be combined to research image reproduction in literary essay translation. Although different gestalt principles and translation techniques are employed, they can achieve aesthetic selection of lexical items, aesthetic harmony of structure and the consistency of aesthetic experience.

5.2 Limitations of the Study

Since gestalt principles and the theory of image-G actualization are seldom combined in previous research on literary translation, the present study is confronted with great difficulties. Also, the limited length and experience of research increase the toughness, resulting in the following limitations of the present study.

To begin with, the examples are mainly selected from literary essays depicting scenes, objects, persons and events where images are abundant in the texts. However, argumentative writing may also contain images. In other words, the images analyzed by the present study are typical but not comprehensive.

What's more, due to limited length in example analysis in Chapter Four, the present study cannot demonstrate all the underlying gestalt principles in the image transference in every literary essay. Therefore, the comparison of similarities and differences between C-E and E-C literary translation are typical results, revealing insufficiency.

CHAPTER FIVE
CONCLUSION

Last but not least, since the present study focuses on the combination of gestalt principles and the theory of image-G actualization as well as the comparison between C-E and E-C translation from the perspective of gestalt, it doesn't expound on the strategies employed by outstanding translators. Instead, it incorporates their techniques in the analysis in Chapter Four.

5.3 Suggestions for Future Study

This book conducts a tentative research on the image reproduction of literary essay translation from the perspective of gestalt at lexical, structural and aesthetic experience levels, exploring the aesthetic effects and making a comparison based on them between C-E and E-C literary essay translation. It is a preliminary exploration that combines gestalt principles with the theory of image-G actualization to study literary essay translation. The translator's strategies are not specifically expounded. Future study can illustrate the translator's strategies from the combined gestalt approach to improve literary essay translation from this perspective. What's more, future study can also involve images in argumentative writing to ensure the diversity of texts.

REFERENCES

Arnheim, R. (1954). *Art and Visual Perception: A Psychology of the Creative Eye.* Berkeley and Los Angeles: University of California Press.

Bell, R. T. (1991). *Translation and Translating: Theory and Practice.* London: Longman Group UK Limited.

Belloc, H. (1931). *On Translation.* Oxford: Clarendon.

Chang, Y. X. [常耀信] (1990). 美国文学简史. 天津: 南开大学出版社.

Chen, G. [陈刚] & Li, G. H. [黎根红] (2008). 格式塔意象重构: 话剧翻译美学之维. 浙江大学学报(人文社会科学版), (1): 183—190.

Chevalier, T. (1997). *Encyclopedia of the Essay.* London & Chicago: Fitzroy Dearborn Publishers.

Eliot, T. S. (1954). *Literary Essays of Ezra Pound.* London: Faber & Faber.

REFERENCES

Evans, V. & Green, M. (2006). *Cognitive Linguistics: An Introduction*. Edinburgh: Edinburgh University Press.

Farahzad, F. (1998). A gestalt approach to manipulation. *Perspectives: Studies in Translatology*, (2): 153–158.

Feng, Q. H. [冯庆华](2002). 文体翻译论. 上海: 上海外语教育出版社.

Gao, J. [高健](2008). 英美散文名篇精华[*A Collection of British and American Essays*]. 上海: 华东师范大学出版社.

Hatim, B. & Mason, I. (2001). *Discourse and the Translator*. Shanghai: Shanghai Foreign Language Education Press.

Holmes, J. S. (1978). Describing literary translation: Models and methods. In Holmes, J. S. et al. (Eds.). *Literature and Translation: New Perspectives in Literary Studies*: 69–82. Leuven: Acco.

Huai, Y. P. [淮亚鹏](2010). 试论散文英译意象再造——格式塔心理学视角. 河南大学.

Huang, J. L. [黄建玲](2012). 美学角度下培根散文汉译的比较研究. 曲阜师范大学.

Jiang, D. D. [姜丹丹](2011). 奈达功能对等理论指导下的汉语现代散文英译研究. 河北师范大学.

Jiang, Q. X. [姜秋霞](2002). 文学翻译中的审美过程: 格

式塔意象再造 [Aesthetic Progression in Literary Translation: Image-G Actualization]. 北京：商务印书馆.

Jiang, Q. X. [姜秋霞] & Quan, X. H. [权晓辉] (2000). 文学翻译过程与格式塔意象模式. 中国翻译, (1): 26—30.

Klein, L. (2015). Same difference: Xi Chuan's *Notes on the Mosquito* and the translation of poetry, prose poetry, and prose. *Translation Review*, (1): 41–50.

Koffka, K. (1928). *The Growth of the Mind: An Introduction to Childpsychology*. 2nd ed. rev. R. M. Ogden (Trans.). London: Kegan Paul, Trench, Trubner & Company.

Koffka, K. (1935). *Principles of Gestalt Psychology*. London: Routledge and Kegan Paul Ltd.

Köhler, W. (1947). *Gestalt Psychology: An Introduction to Modern Psychology*. New York: Liveright Pub. Corp.

Lai, X. P. [赖晓鹏] (2009). 从翻译美学的角度看张培基《英译中国现代散文选》(三辑) 的审美再现. 华中师范大学.

Lefevere, A. (2004). *Translation, Rewriting and Manipulation of Literary Fame*. Shanghai: Shanghai Foreign Language Education Press.

REFERENCES

Li, C. B. [黎昌抱] (2008). 王佐良翻译风格研究. 上海外国语大学.

Liu, S. C. [刘士聪] (2002). 汉英英汉美文翻译与鉴赏 [*Prose Translation and Appreciation*]. 南京: 译林出版社.

Liu, Z. D. [刘重德] (1991). 文学翻译十讲. 北京: 中国对外翻译出版公司.

Ma, D. Z. [马德忠] (2006). 英语散文汉译的翻译标准——忠实、通顺、美. 天津理工大学.

Ma, J. [麻锦] & Jia, D. J. [贾德江] (2011). 试论译文读者在现代散文汉英翻译中的地位. 内蒙古农业大学学报(社会科学版), (6): 370—374.

Mao, R. G. [毛荣贵] (2005). 翻译美学. 上海: 上海交通大学出版社.

Meng, J. [孟瑾] & Feng, D. [冯斗] (2005). 古诗格式塔意象和意境的传递. 外语学刊, (4): 91—94.

Meng, L. [孟立] (2004). 中国古典诗词中的意象及其翻译. 上海外国语大学.

Miller, E. G. (1986). *The Dynamic of the Re-creative Process in Translation: Hugo Lindo's Poetry*. Ann Arbor: University Microfilms International.

Neubert, A. & Shreve, M. G. (1992). *Translation as Text*.

Kent: The Kent State University Press.

Niu, R. [牛蕊] & Chen, S. S. [陈珊珊] (2009). 意象翻译过程中格式塔心理学的应用. 陕西教育学院学报, (1): 84—87.

Pan, W. M. [潘卫民] (2006). 景点英译的格式塔诠释. 中国科技翻译, (4): 44—47.

Peng, F. S. [彭发胜] (2016). 主语驱动原则下的汉语散文英译策略研究. 外语教学与研究(外国语文双月刊), (1): 128—138.

Pollard, D. [卜立德] (1989). 英国随笔与中国现代散文. 中国现代文学研究丛刊, (3): 81—98.

Pollard, D. (2002). *The Chinese Essay*. New York: Columbia University Press.

Qian, L. J. [钱灵杰] & Cao, P. [操萍] (2011). 刘炳善散文翻译思想研究. 广东外语外贸大学学报, (2): 89—92.

Rock, I. & Palmer, S. (1990). The legacy of gestalt psychology. *Scientific American*, (6): 84-90.

Shi, M. L. [石梅琳] (2015). 读者反映论视角下《落花生》三英译本比较研究. 吉林大学.

Snell-Hornby, M. (1995). *Translation Studies: An Integrated Approach*. Amsterdam/Philadelphia: John Benjamins Pub. Co.

REFERENCES

Su, C. (2017). An applied study to image-G transmission in Chinese literary on gestalt perception laws. *Open Journal of Modern Linguistics*, (7): 272–289.

Sun, H. F. [孙会芳] (2009). 张培基、刘士聪散文翻译风格对比研究. 中南大学.

Tang, P. [唐萍] (2015). 文化介入视角下张培基英译中国现代散文批评研究. 信阳师范学院.

Tang, Y. C. [唐耀彩] (2001). 散文翻译中的跨句法——兼评张培基《英译中国现代散文选》. 北京第二外国语学院学报, (4): 57—62, 86.

Todorovic, D. (2008). Gestalt principles. In *Scholarpedia Journal Vol. 12*. San Diego: Scholarpedia.

Tong, Y. [童莹] & Gu, F. R. [顾飞荣] (2008). 翻译研究的格式塔视角. 南京农业大学学报(社会科学版), (2): 109—112.

Wang, B. [王冰] (2014). 夏济安散文翻译风格研究——以夏译《美国名家散文选读》为例. 广东外语外贸大学.

Wang, J. P. [王建平] (2005). 汉诗英译中的格式塔艺术空白处理. 外语学刊, (4): 84—90.

Wang, J. [王军] (2010). 翻译普遍性和张培基的《英译中国现代散文选》研究. 东华大学.

Wang, X. J. [王小婧] (2013). 关联理论视角下夏济安《名家散文选读》翻译策略解析. 上海外国语大学.

Wang, Y. [王寅] (1990). 英汉语言宏观结构区别特征. 外国语, (6): 24—40.

Wertheimer, M. (1912). Experimentelle Studien über das Sehen von Bewegung [Experimental studies on the perception of motion]. *Zeitschrift für Psychologie*, (1): 161–265.

Wu, D. L. [吴迪龙] & Zhu, X. L. [朱献珑] (2008). 格式塔理论观照下的科技英语含义. 华东交通大学学报, (2): 74—77.

Wu, J. B. [吴剑波] (2012). 从及物性理论看英语抒情散文的汉译. 新疆师范大学.

Xia, J. A. [夏济安] (2000). 美国名家散文选读 [*A Collection of American Essays*]. 上海: 复旦大学出版社.

Xia, T. D. [夏廷德] & Ma, Z. B. [马志波] (2008). 英语散文翻译的声律再现问题. 大连海事大学学报(社会科学版), (3): 168—170.

Xin, C. H. [辛春晖] (2005). 谈译文的形式与内容——比较张培基和张梦井翻译的朱自清散文《匆匆》. 长春大学学报, (5): 43—46.

Yu, D. [余东] & Liu, S. C. [刘士聪] (2014). 论散文翻译

REFERENCES

中的节奏. 中国翻译,(2):92—96.

Zhang, J. C.[张嘉晨](2008). 散文翻译中名词复数汉译策略研究. 知识经济,(1):137,140.

Zhang, J. G.[张继光] & Zhang, Z.[张政](2014). 基于语料库的当代英语散文汉译规范研究[J]. 外语教学理论与实践,(4):83—91.

Zhang, P. J.[张培基](2007). 英译中国现代散文选(一)(二)(三)(四)[Selected Modern Chinese Essays]. 上海:上海外语教育出版社.

Zhang, S. Y.[张思永](2011). 焦菊隐"整体观"翻译思想的现代阐释——格式塔心理学视角. 北京第二外国语学院学报,(8):19—24.

Zhang, W. Q.[张文清](2007). 张培基的翻译思想研究. 福建师范大学.

Zhang, X. H.[张晓宏](2011). 从格式塔意象再造看英语散文翻译的审美再现——以夏济安《名家散文选读》为例. 北京语言大学.

Zhao, X. M.[赵秀明] & Zhao, Z. J.[赵张进](2010). 英美散文研究与翻译. 长春:吉林大学出版社.

Zhao, Y. L.[赵亚力](2009). 从译者主体性看张培基散文翻译——兼评《英译中国现代散文选》. 合肥工业大学.

Zhou, T.［周涛］(2004). 散文翻译的美学建构——评夏译散文《古屋杂忆》. 咸宁学院学报, (5): 131—134.

Zhu, G. C.［朱桂成］(2008). 格式塔心理学下的翻译理论假说. 江苏外语教学研究, (2): 67—72.

后 记

  2011年9月,刚进入江南大学读本科的我并没有立志学术,但英语专业很多课程的小班化教学令我掌握了较为扎实的基础知识,且受益匪浅。大四刚开学时我有幸顺利保研。虽然这相当于提前一年进入研究生阶段,但由于对理论掌握不够透彻等原因,我的本科毕业论文差强人意。2015年9月正式开始研究生学习后,我在第一年的学习中重新寻找选题灵感。翻译、语言学、文学方向的课程不仅让我更加系统地掌握了三个方向的基础知识,认知语言学课程更是将这一前沿方向进行了详细介绍。认知语言学将认知心理学这一相邻学科中的理论与语言学相结合,提出了很多创新性的概念,大多被运用于语言学研究,尤其是其中的格式塔心理学原则还可以应用于文学翻译研究。在科研方法课程学习中,老师从如何确定研究问题、阅读和整理文献、撰写文献综述,到研究方法、过程和结论,系统地将论文撰写的方法教授给我们,同时不忘布置阶段性的课程任务,以巩固学习成果。这两门课程的难度相对较大,在学习和完成阶段性任务的过程中,我不仅在学术上有了较大的进步,也能静下心来认真研读文献,为我的论文写作打下了坚实的基础。

经过导师的指导和斟酌,论文选题的确定比较顺利。以格式塔心理学为切入点查找与文学翻译有关的文献,我很快发现了格式塔意象这一概念。它是格式塔心理学原则的一小部分应用于文学翻译的成果,因此我尝试将二者结合起来。后来我发现它们在诗歌翻译中的应用较多,散文翻译中的应用较少。因此,我将散文作为研究对象,选题定为"格式塔理论视角下散文翻译中的意象再现研究"。这一阶段主要阅读相关文献的摘要以了解研究现状,但接下来仔细研读了两本专著《文学翻译中的审美过程:格式塔意象再造》和 Principles of Gestalt Psychology,详细学习其中理论内容的过程比较漫长和辛苦。两本专著的难度很大,开题前四个月开始研读时,第一遍只能断断续续地勉强读完,读了书评后再读一遍专著,才能掌握理论的主要内容。开题完成后第三遍研读专著时,我才真正发现了格式塔意象与格式塔心理学原则的交叉点,即格式塔意象是基于格式塔心理学的完形趋向律法则发展而来的,格式塔心理学原则可以用来解释格式塔意象再造的心理过程。对几个系列中

后记

英文对照散文选的研读也充满了挑战。一开始,我发现张培基译注的《英译中国现代散文选》和夏济安译的《美国名家散文选读》是散文翻译研究的热点对象,但为了验证格式塔理论在翻译研究中应用的普适性,又增加了卜立德译的《古今散文英译集》、高健译注的《英美散文名篇精华》和刘士聪编著的《汉英英汉美文翻译与鉴赏》,研究对象的体量很大,给主体部分的例证分析带来了比较大的困难。首先是框架结构难以决定。研究对象从中译英、英译中各一个系列散文选变成了各两个系列,刘士聪的《汉英英汉美文翻译与鉴赏》更是包含中译英和英译中两个方向,打乱了原本的分析框架。我尝试着按照每篇散文的类别来分析后发现结构会变得十分复杂,于是在导师的建议下,我采用中译英、英译中两个大方向下再细分为词汇、结构和审美体验三个层面的分析框架。其次是典型例证的寻找变得困难。三个层面上的分析需要例证的支持,研究对象体量的增大丰富了文章内容的同时,也加大了论文的工作量。最后,结论归纳也比较困难。文章将格式塔心理学原则与格式塔意象再造理论相结合,以五本中英对照散文选为研究对象,从中译英和英译中两个方向,研究散文翻译中的意象再现,并从格式塔理论角度对比散文中译英和英译中时意象再现的异同,涵盖的内容较多,对比分析时既要呈现中译英和英译中

两个方向在格式塔心理学原则应用上的异同,又要呈现它们在语言表现形式上的异同,用文字无法描述清楚,于是借助表格,以便清楚地表达。

在江南大学读研的三年,我不仅在学业上大有进益,也在实践中找到了自己的职业方向。第一学年的学业课程结束后,在第二、第三学年我有充足的时间沉淀下来做学术,参加实践,磨炼出了冷静的性格,就像培根所说的"凡有所学,皆成性格"。很多人觉得读研的意义不大,但我在江南大学读研得到的不仅是学历,更是能力与性格的成长。

从大一到研三,在江南大学七年的学习生活精彩而快乐。外国语学院本科的小班化教学不仅保证了教学质量,也保证了学习质量,丰富的课程活动还锻炼了我的演讲能力和视频制作技能;研究生专业化的课程及前沿讲座更是让我找到了毕业论文选题灵感,发现了自己的学术潜能。学校的食、住、行都很便捷,图书馆的现代化设施能满足自习、研讨、朗读的需要,是朋友眼中"别人家的图书馆"。目前我已毕业一年,经历了本科的顺风顺水、研究生每个阶段完成的不同任务,带着从母校七年学习生活中获得的技能和培养的性格,继续在工作岗位上认真学习新的知识,积极适应身份的转变。虽然在近期不会接触学术研究,但硕士论文撰写时养成的严谨态度和掌握的学术技能一定会在今

后记

后的工作中发挥积极作用。

在此,感谢我的导师龚晓斌教授对我的辛勤付出,没有他的谆谆教导和学术引导,我不可能很顺利地完成研究生阶段的学习。他的跨学科学术视野(语言学、翻译学、文体学等学科的交融)和严谨细致的作风(例如最后阶段对于论文标题的反复推敲)都给我留下了深刻的印象。感谢七年来江南大学外国语学院老师对我的栽培,愿母校的明天更加美好。

李 梦
2019年6月于江苏宜兴